WRITE THIS BOOK

A-Do-It-Yourself Mystery

Written by
You

with the reluctant assistance of
pseudonymous bosch

Illustrations by Gilbert Ford

LITTLE, BROWN AND COMPANY
New York Boston

SUGGESTED TITLES
The Best Book Ever Written
The Book That's Going to Make Me Famous
Buy This Book, You Won't Regret It
Like a Video Game, Only More Awesome
Read and Be Amazed
I Just Wrote This Book, What Have You Done?
Harry Potter and the _ _ _ _ _ _ _ _ _ _ *

SUGGESTED PSEUDONYMS
Dr. Seuss
Mark Twain
Lewis Carroll
Anne Ominus
Pseudonymous Bosch

---

*HEY, IT WORKED IN THE PAST. AND I'LL TELL YOU A SECRET—TITLES CAN'T BE COPYRIGHTED. YOU CAN STEAL ANY TITLE YOU LIKE, EVEN ONE OF MINE.

ALTERNATIVE TITLE PAGE

If you don't like *Write This Book*—and, really, what kind of title is that?—then please write your own title here.*

_ _ _ _ _ _ _ _ _ _ _ _ _ _ _ _ _ _

_ _ _ _ _ _ _ _ _ _ _ _ _ _ _ _ _

Written by

_ _ _ _ _ _ _ _ _ _ _ _ _ _ _ _

Choose your pseudonym or, as I prefer to call it, your *nom de plume*. Or really confuse everybody and use your real name!**

---

*HERE AND THROUGHOUT THIS BOOK, YOU MIGHT CONSIDER WRITING IN PENCIL RATHER THAN PEN. THAT WAY YOU CAN ERASE YOUR TRACKS, SO TO SPEAK. LIBRARIANS ESPECIALLY CAN GET RATHER PEEVISH WHEN THEY SEE PEN MARKS IN THEIR BOOKS.

**IF YOU HAVE ENGAGED IN ANY CRIMINAL ADVENTURES INVOLVING DUPLICITOUS SCHEMES AND HIDDEN IDENTITIES—THAT IS TO SAY, IF YOU HAVE READ ANY OF MY PREVIOUS BOOKS—THEN YOU KNOW WHAT A PSEUDONYM IS: THE PART OF MY NAME THAT COMES BEFORE *OUS*. MORE GENERALLY, IT IS A NAME AN AUTHOR USES WHEN HE IS TOO SCARED TO PUT HIS OWN NAME ON A BOOK.

COPYRIGHT PAGE*

Don't copy me! That's what a copyright page is saying. Just as you might say to your little brother when he says he likes the same flavor ice cream you do. A copyright is literally the right to copy—and/or publish—a book. Usually, the author of a book holds the copyright. However, in the case of this book, you are the author and *I* hold the copyright. It's very unfair when you think about it. Don't think about it.

DEDICATION PAGE*

Circle all that apply.

This book is dedicated to:

a) everyone who said I
would never write a book

b) my future fans

c) my language arts teacher
(can't hurt, right?)

d) the highest bidder

e) me, because who am I
really writing this book
for, after all?

*AS YOU KNOW, THE DEDICATION PAGE IS BY FAR THE MOST IMPORTANT PAGE OF ANY BOOK. IT IS YOUR CHANCE TO REWARD FRIENDS, PUNISH ENEMIES, AND MAKE EVERYONE ELSE JEALOUS AND RESENTFUL. MY ADVICE IS TO FILL IN THIS PAGE LAST, BECAUSE THE PERSON YOU WANT TO DEDICATE YOUR BOOK TO TODAY MAY BE THE PERSON YOU WANT TO FLING THE BOOK AT TOMORROW. ALSO, BY KEEPING THE DEDICATION PAGE OPEN, YOU CAN ALWAYS DANGLE THE POSSIBILITY OF A DEDICATION IN THE FACES OF YOUR SCHOOLMATES AND GET THEM TO GIVE YOU THEIR DESSERTS AT LUNCHTIME.

EPIGRAPH*

Choose one or more:

The birth of the reader must be at the cost
of the death of the Author.
—*Roland Barthes*

The index of a book should always be written
by the author, even though the book itself
should be the work of another hand.
—*Mark Twain*

O CHILD LEARN YOUR ABZ'S
AND MEMORIZE THEM WELL
AND YOU SHALL LEARN TO TALK AND THINK
AND READ AND WRITE AND SPEL.
—*Shel Silverstein*

Xx xx xx xxx xx xx xxxx xx xxx xxxxxxxx.
—*Xxxxxxxxxxxx Xxxxx*

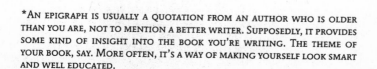

*AN EPIGRAPH IS USUALLY A QUOTATION FROM AN AUTHOR WHO IS OLDER
THAN YOU ARE, NOT TO MENTION A BETTER WRITER. SUPPOSEDLY, IT PROVIDES
SOME KIND OF INSIGHT INTO THE BOOK YOU'RE WRITING. THE THEME OF
YOUR BOOK, SAY. MORE OFTEN, IT'S A WAY OF MAKING YOURSELF LOOK SMART
AND WELL EDUCATED.

TABLE OF CONTENTS*

*FRANKLY, THE TERM *TABLE OF CONTENTS* HAS NEVER MADE MUCH SENSE TO ME. A BOX HAS CONTENTS. A BOOK HAS WORDS. IT DOESN'T CONTAIN ANYTHING. AS FOR A TABLE, IT DOESN'T HAVE ANY CONTENTS, EITHER; IT HAS...A TOP...LEGS...MAYBE A FEW LOOSE SCREWS. YES, I KNOW, A TABLE OF CONTENTS IS NOT A TABLE AS IN DINNER TABLE; IT'S A TABLE AS IN MULTIPLICATION TABLE. BUT THAT ONLY MULTIPLIES THE PROBLEM. AND MY MATH IS TERRIBLE. I THINK I'LL TABLE THIS DISCUSSION RIGHT NOW.

FOREWORD*

IMAGINE YOU'RE READING A BOOK.

It's a far-fetched idea, I realize, but indulge me for a moment.

What's that? You want to know *what* you are reading?

You're reading a book. Like this one. You know, with sentences. And paragraphs. That sort of thing.

Where are you reading? Oh, on a plane? On a train? Hanging upside down? Wherever you want.

So, as I was saying, you're reading this book and—

Why are you reading? Aaargh. Who's the writer here, anyway? (Well, actually, that's the question I'm getting to, but be patient.) Maybe you're reading for school. Or maybe you're reading because your parent is paying you. (Now, *there*'s a good reason to read a book.) Or maybe you're reading for fun. Because you *like* to *read*. It is possible.**

Now, please, don't interrupt again.

---

*WHAT IS A *FOREWORD*? WHY, IT'S THE OPPOSITE OF A *BACKWORD*, OF COURSE. AH, BUT THERE'S NO SUCH WORD AS *BACKWORD*, ONLY *BACKWARD*. AND YOU DON'T SAY *A BACKWARD*, ANYWAY. (UNLESS YOU'RE TALKING ABOUT THE BACK OF THE WARD—YOU KNOW, WHERE THEY KEEP THE *REALLY* CRAZY PEOPLE.) YOU'RE RIGHT; I WAS JOKING. A FOREWORD IS A SECTION AT THE FRONT OF A BOOK WHERE YOU ARE LIKELY TO FIND SOMETHING ABOUT THE ORIGINS OF OR INSPIRATION FOR THE BOOK. BUT THAT DOESN'T SOUND NEARLY AS ORIGINAL OR INSPIRED, DOES IT?

**IF YOU'RE ONE OF THOSE PEOPLE WHO HAVE THEIR HEADS IN A BOOK ALL THE TIME—IF YOU'RE A READER, A REAL READER, IN OTHER WORDS—TAKE HEART. I WAS JUST LIKE YOU ONCE—AND LOOK HOW I ENDED UP! FRIENDLESS. ALONE. WRITING NONSENSICAL BOOKS THAT DRIVE PEOPLE LIKE YOU INSANE.

Imagine you're reading a book. *Whatever* book. In *whatever* location. For *whatever* reason.

Somehow you manage to get through the first few sentences without falling asleep. You're even a little bit intrigued. A little bit. Mildly.

Before you know it, you've read a whole page. Then two pages. The book is starting to grab you because it's funny or scary or mysterious. Or because the main character reminds you of somebody you know. Or because it's about your favorite subject—chocolate. (Well, my favorite, anyway.) Or maybe you don't know why you like the book. It doesn't matter—you're on a reading roll! You consider bragging online about it, or rewarding yourself with a snack, or ascending to the next level on the video game you were playing a moment before. But you decide to stick with it a moment longer. After all, your parent is paying you, right? (I knew that was it!) You'll read another page or two before calling it a night.

So you turn the page, you read another sentence, and then...nothing. The words just drop off.

Like t

h

i

s

(Imagine this page is completely blank.)

(This one, too.)

(And one more, just for the heck of it.)

(Well, you get the idea.)

Frantically, you flip pages.
Almost the entire book is blank.
What is going on? What happened to the story? What kind of book is this?
You start to feel angry. You want your money back. (So what if you checked out the book from the library—the library had to pay for it, right?) Let's see, what did this book cost? What else could

you have bought with that princely sum? How many movie tickets? How many candy bars? All that for the price of one so-called book without any writing in it? What a rip!

Well, I have bad news to share with you: something like that happens in this book. Not just once. Over and over again. A certain author, whom I won't name (okay, me), has abandoned his book and has left his readers hanging out to dry. This is a crime, I admit, almost on a par with abandoning your child. Or even your lunch. But there it is. Most of this book, well, I just haven't written it. And I'm not going to, either.

Why? Oh, I have my reasons. Big. Grown-up. Author. Reasons. Unfortunately, I can't reveal them yet. Let's just say a life is at stake (mine) and leave it at that.

I know, you're steaming mad, and you have every right to be, but before you toss this book in the trash, consider my message to you:

DIY

No, silly. Not *DIE*. (I want you alive, but, please, no kicking.) *D—I—Y. Do it yourself.* I'm offering you the opportunity to write this book yourself.

That's right, you. You, the poor person unlucky enough to pick up this useless pile of words. I'm sorry, I mean you, the clever person lucky enough to pick up this delightful piece of prose!

You, the reader of this book, shall be the author of this book.

Think about what that means: an entire world under your control. Heroes and heroines, action and adventure, laughter and tears—all yours for the taking...or, rather, for the making. There might be dragons or unicorns or ninjas or zombies or cockroaches. And those are just the people you know. Wait until you get to invent new stuff! This could be fun. It *should* be fun. In my experience, the more fun you have writing, the more fun your reader will have reading.

Dragon   Unicorn   Ninja

Zombie   Cockroach

What do you say?

Haven't you ever wanted to write a book? I can't tell you how many letters I get from readers asking for advice about writing. *Where do you get your ideas? What makes a good story? How do I get published?* Well, here it is—a book written by you that's *already published.*

Not everybody's as vain as you are, P.B. You can't buy people off so easily!

Sorry, that's my pet rabbit assistant, Quiche. Ignore him.

Just think: it's *your* book. With *your* name on it. You can even put *your* picture on the back.

I'll tell you what: to sweeten the deal, I will give you a few helpful hints. I might even write a chapter or two for you. Three, I'll write three chapters. This won't be hard—well, not very hard, I promise. And who knows? You might even learn something about writing while you're at it.

Learn something from YOU?

So, my dear reader and (I hope) writer, can I assume you're in?

What's that? You want to know what the book's about before you commit to writing it?

Shh! Nobody's listening to you, Quiche!

Hmm. Normally, I wouldn't tell you about a book before you read it. That's what's called spoiling the plot, and in my world it's a capital offense. However, if you're going to write this book, I suppose it's only fair that I give you an idea.

The book is a mystery about a missing author, I.B. Anonymous—a writer of mysteries for young readers who abandons a manuscript before it's finished. Sound familiar?*

Where has this mysterious author gone? Ah, that I cannot tell you. Is I.B. dead or alive? Is he on the run from the law? Is he in a witness protection program? Was he kidnapped? Abducted by aliens?

*As you probably guessed, *I.B. Anonymous* is a pseudonym. A pseudonym for a pseudonym. Which makes it a *pseudopseudonym*. Which is like the double negative of names. Which means . . . almost nothing at all.**

By the way, the little note above this one? That's a footnote. So is the note you're reading. This is a footnote to a footnote . . . about footnotes. What is a footnote? Well, it's not a note written on your foot, if that's what you're thinking. Neither is it a note written *with* your foot. A footnote is simply a note on the bottom— or foot, get it?—of a page. As you've had the misfortune of reading any of my previous books, a footnote explains or elaborates on something that is written above it. Usually, footnotes are indicated by a number or a star or stars (plural) like these *. When you see the number or star or stars (plural), you're supposed to look down to the bottom of the page. Yes, you should look down now.

***Ha. Made you look.

As the new author of this book, you have to figure out what happened to the old author. Without you, he will never be found. The story will never be told, and the book will never be finished.

Think of it this way: this book is a mystery novel—but this time the mystery is the novel itself. It's an inside-out mystery. Call it *The Case of the Missing Author*.

Your job is to solve it.

Good luck.

—P.B.

PREFACE*

Your chance to add a few words before we begin:

— — — — — — — — — — — — —

— — — — — — — — — — — — —

— — — — — — — — — — — — —

— — — — — — — — — — — — —

— — — — — — — — — — — — —

— — — — — — — — — — — — —

— — — — — — — — — — — — —

— — — — — — — — — — — — —

— — — — — — — — — — — — —

— — — — — — — — — — — — —

— — — — — — — — — — — — —

*A PREFACE USUALLY SAYS SOMETHING ABOUT A BOOK'S ORIGINS OR INSPIRA-
TION. AS YOU MAY RECALL, A FOREWORD USUALLY SAYS SOMETHING ABOUT A
BOOK'S ORIGINS OR INSPIRATION, AS WELL; AND I'VE ALREADY WRITTEN A
FOREWORD TO THIS BOOK. THEREFORE, YOU'RE FREE TO WRITE ANYTHING YOU
LIKE HERE. IF YOU MUST HAVE A TOPIC, YOU MIGHT TRY WRITING ABOUT YOUR
BIGGEST FEARS ABOUT WRITING THIS BOOK—SO THAT I WILL KNOW HOW BEST
TO FRIGHTEN YOU IN THE UPCOMING PAGES.

CHAPTER ONE

Beginnings: The Blank Page

Enough with the epigraphs and dedications! It's time to start writing this book in earnest. Ready?

One...

Two...

Three...

What happened? You're sure not writing very fast.

Scary, isn't it? A blank page staring you in the face.

Luckily, that's just a drawing. Pages don't really stare at you; you stare at them. It follows that a blank page should be scared of you, not the other way around. Feel better?

Good. Now get to it—

What? Still having trouble?

Oh, I forgot. Here are some lines to help guide your handwriting:

Don't tell me, you want straight lines. So fussy! It's not the lines? You don't know what to write? I hope you're not just procrastinating.*

OK, OK, I'll write the first chapter. But please, dear reader, don't get used to it. You are going to have to take the wheel soon—even if you don't have a driver's license. In fact, let's not call it a chapter;

*ACCORDING TO THE DICTIONARY DEFINITION, WE PROCRASTINATORS ARE PEOPLE WHO HABITUALLY POSTPONE DOING THINGS, BUT I PREFER TO THINK OF US AS *PRO CRASTINATORS*—IN OTHER WORDS, PROFESSIONAL CRASTINATORS. WHAT IS A CRASTINATOR? OH, I'LL TELL YOU LATER.

let's call it a prologue. That way I won't feel like I'm doing so much work.*

At the beginning of a book, many writers, especially lazy writers like me, try to grab their readers with a quick action-oriented teaser, like you might see on a crime show on TV. This is hack writing of the highest order. And it's exactly what I'm going to attempt here.

Now pay attention. This is the beginning of your very own book.

The Case of the Missing Author
Prologue

It all began with a laugh, a cry, and a thud. The laugh was so loud it—

What, you're stopping me already? Oh, you think *It all began with* is a dull way to begin, do you?

At least you'll admit that the laugh-cry-thud combo creates a compelling sense of mystery....

No? The only mystery is why I'm such a bad writer that it makes you want to laugh and cry at once?

---

*CONFUSED ABOUT THE DIFFERENCES BETWEEN A FOREWORD, A PREFACE, AND A PROLOGUE? IF IT'S ANY CONSOLATION, I AM, TOO.

Pseudo-intelligence:
First sentence or death sentence?

Let's face it: most readers will never get past your first sentence. You may as well make it a good one. But how? Many writers slave over their opening sentences, trying to come up with something profound. (*Happy twelve-year-olds are all alike; every unhappy twelve-year-old is unhappy in his own way.*) Other writers make desperate attempts to create a compelling, er, sense of mystery. (Like, say, *It all began with a laugh, a cry, and a thud.*) Still others try to make their first sentences look exactly like all their other sentences; in other words, they try very hard to make it look like they didn't try very hard. (For instance... actually, it's hard to think of one of those because, well, they sound just like other sentences.) As for *your* first sentence, my advice is to come up with a few, then choose which one you like best. Chances are you'll be able to use all of them eventually. If you can't think of a decent first sentence, write your second sentence. Or third. Or last. Don't let your first sentence turn into a death sentence.*

*FOR A FEW FAMOUS EXAMPLES OF OPENING SENTENCES, CHECK THE BACK OF THIS BOOK.

You're a hoot. Where did you get that joke from—my genius rabbit? I'll tell you what, smarty-pants, why don't we keep my first sentence—temporarily—as a placeholder, then you can insert your vastly better sentence at a later time. Fair enough?

STORE YOUR FIRST SENTENCE HERE FOR LATER USE:

— — — — — — — — — — — — — — — —

— — — — — — — — — — — — — — —

— — — — — — — — — — — — — — —

— — — — — — — — — — — — — — —

Now, with your permission, I will begin again. Read closely—this is your chance to see a master writer at work! And yes, by *master writer* I am referring to myself.

The Case of the Missing Author
Prologue

It all began with a laugh, a cry, and a thud. The laugh was so loud it made Z_____ sit up in bed. It came from across the street and it sounded like the laugh of a madman. It gave him the creeps.

Before Z_____ could lie back down, the laugh was replaced by a desperate, piercing cry. The cry of a wounded animal. Or of a man reduced to the state of an animal.

The cry was followed by a thud so heavy it could have been a boulder falling to the floor.

Or a dead body.

Z_____ ran into his sister's room. A drastic measure reserved strictly for emergencies.

"A_____, wake up."

"Go away." A_____ tried to bury her head in her pillow, but Z_____ gave her a hard sh—

If this is supposed to be so educational, Mr.—cough—Master Writer, why don't you talk about how you're setting up your characters and their relationship?

Because I thought it was obvious, Mr.—cough—Assistant! Z_____ doesn't like his sister. Or she's very strict about not letting him into her room. Or her room is so messy it's dangerous. Or—well, the point is, all that stuff will be decided later. I'm being purposefully, er...

Vague and confusing?

Yes...no! Now you're confusing me.

"Go away." A____ tried to bury her head in her pillow, but Z____ gave her a hard shake.

"It's important."

"What is?"

He told her what he'd heard.

She cocked her head, listening. All was silent now. "And you're sure it was *him*?" She gestured in the direction of the house across the street.

"Uh-huh. C'mon—we have to do something!"

Grumpily, A____ followed Z____ downstairs.

Hearts beating fast, they cracked open the front door and peeked out. There was a full moon and they could see as clearly as if it were daytime. And yet there was nothing to see. The house across the street looked completely peaceful.

A____ stared at it, more curious than she'd let on. Their new neighbor had moved in two months earlier. They knew next to nothing about him, only that he was supposed to be some kind of author—a profession that might be suspicious in the eyes of some but that intrigued her greatly.

There. Now you know their neighbor is an author. (Did you guess that this author is I.B. himself? Then you're one step ahead.) You see how I'm weaving in crucial information without interrupting the flow of the story?

In other words, you're interrupting your story to tell us you're not interrupting your story....

You're the one who told me to!

"Maybe he was reading one of his books out loud," A____ suggested. "I heard writers do that."*

"It wasn't words; it was a laugh, and then a scream, and then—"

"So what do you want to do? Knock on his door?"

Z____ shrugged unhappily. He didn't know what he wanted to do.

"He won't let anyone in during the daytime," A____ continued. "Can you imagine how mad he would be if somebody barged in on him in the middle of the night?"

"He won't be mad if he's dead."

---

*She's not wrong; many writers read their words aloud. It's a great way to figure out what works and what needs cutting. Needless to say, I rarely do this myself. I prefer to write as I live—in ignorance.

A____ rolled her eyes. "Maybe he was watching a sitcom and that was the laugh you heard. Then he switched to a horror movie—"

"And then what—he knocked the TV over?"

"Why not? Aren't all writers supposed to be crazy?"

Z____ laughed, his mind turning to the mystery series he was reading: A Series of Secrets by I.B. Anonymous. If their neighbor's books were anything like I.B.'s, then their neighbor must be completely nuts.

His sister was right, thought Z____: in a writer's house, sounds didn't necessarily mean what you thought they did.

Remembering all the twists and turns and zany reveals in I.B.'s secret stories, Z____ allowed A____ to lead him back upstairs.

This neighbor guy does sound familiar....

Shortly afterward, the door of their neighbor's house opened, and a pair of eyes peered out into the night. Satisfied that he/she/it wasn't being watched, the owner of those eyes crept out of the house.

A moment later, he/she/it had vanished.

Out of the distance came the sound of a dog—or was it a wolf?—howling at the moon.

Department of Pitfalls:
His and Hers

A moment later,
he/she/it had vanished.

He/she/it? Did I really write that awkward conjunction of pronouns? You should definitely change it when you revise this book.

There are few problems more perplexing than how to refer to somebody whose gender is unknown. In the case above, I didn't want to give up anything about the identity of the creature exiting the author's house—that's why I wrote what I wrote. But often vagueness is not a matter of choice.

Is my reader a girl or a boy? I don't know. Despite what I may pretend, I can't see you.

He/she, s/he, it, they, them—we well-meaning authors will try everything and anything so as not to exclude anybody. Often, I confess, I give up and simply write *he* or *him* or *his* when what I mean is: *he or she* or *him or her* or *his or hers*. I do this because I am lazy and my well-meaning-ness only goes so far. I do not recommend that you follow my example; undoubtedly, it is unfair to my female readers. Indeed, you should feel free to cross out all my *he*s and *him*s and *his*'s, or at least to add a few *she*s and *her*s and *hers*'s.

His's and hers's? Your writing is getting worse's and worse's!

PROCRASTINATION PAGE

SPEND TEN MINUTES IMAGINING
WHAT YOU WILL WEAR WHEN
YOU'RE A FAMOUS WRITER.*

DECIDE IT'S ALL WRONG.

THINK OF SOMETHING ELSE TO WEAR.

DECIDE IT'S ALL WRONG, TOO.

*EVERY AUTHOR NEEDS A UNIFORM. TOM WOLFE, FOR EXAMPLE, IS KNOWN
FOR WEARING ONLY WHITE SUITS. ANOTHER AUTHOR I CAN THINK OF NEVER
LEAVES HIS HOUSE WITHOUT HIS SUNGLASSES. HE THINKS IT MAKES HIM LOOK
DASHING AND MYSTERIOUS. PLEASE DON'T TELL HIM OTHERWISE.

CHAPTER TWO

Writing Materials:
The *mise en place*

Well, did you like the beginning of your book? Think you can do better?

Good. You can prove it by answering the following:

What happens next?

(Almost all fiction writing boils down to that essential question.)

What—you're not a fortune-teller? You can't see the future?

Very funny. I meant, what happens next in *your story*—not what happens next in your life. You may not be able to *see* the future, but as the author of this book you can *write* it.

You still don't know what happens next?

I don't mean to insult you, but I'm not surprised. It's very difficult to make something from nothing.

Creative freedom is all well and good, but in my

opinion, writing requires a degree of preparation. I feel the same way about dinner. Making dinner, that is. (Eating dinner I'm happy to do quite spontaneously.) Whenever I cook, I try to assemble my ingredients beforehand. I don't want to get halfway through my chocolate chip cookie dough only to discover I've already eaten all the chocolate chips.

Which you usually have!

Watch out, Quiche, or I just might eat you!

The French have a name for this practice of preassembling ingredients, as they do for many crucial culinary activities: the *mise en place*. The *set in place*. To make sure you have all the materials you need for your book, I suggest you create a literary *mise en place*.

What should go into your *mise en place*? Aside from those chocolate chips,

Rhymes with "sneeze on boss"...

of course. (Chocolate, I'm sure you'll agree, is absolutely vital to the writing process.) Well, what is necessary for writing? Let's start with the basics:

- a **writing utensil** (pen, pencil, crayon, feather quill, electronic computational device, lipstick, chocolate-smeared finger)

- a **writing surface** (napkin, table, tablet, chalk-
board, bedroom wall, dusty car window, plaster
cast, old tennis shoe, palm of hand)

- and...**something to write about**
(Ah, now that's the tricky one,
isn't it?)

What about a rabbit slave to type everything for you? You missed that one!

What should you keep by your side to help you
come up with story ideas? One answer is: anything that inspires you.

Feel free to ignore this list and create your own:

- A BAD DREAM
- A GOOD JOKE
- AN OLD COMIC
- A BROKEN TOY
- AN OVERHEARD CONVERSATION
- CHOCOLATE
- MORE CHOCOLATE
- RANDOM FACTS ABOUT BLACK HOLES AND DINOSAURS
- A PICTURE OF YOUR ENEMY WITH A SCRIBBLE MUSTACHE
- A PAGE COPIED FROM YOUR SISTER'S DIARY
- YOUR FATHER'S HAT
- YOUR FAVORITE SHOE
- A LIST OF FUNNY FOREIGN SWEAR WORDS

- A UFO sighting
- A reflective surface
- A diagram of a space station . . . for mice
- And did I mention chocolate?

— — — — — — — — — — — — — — — — — —

— — — — — — — — — — — — — — — — —

— — — — — — — — — — — — — — — — —

— — — — — — — — — — — — — — — — —

— — — — — — — — — — — — — — — —

— — — — — — — — — — — — — — — —

— — — — — — — — — — — — — — — —

— — — — — — — — — — — — — — — —

— — — — — — — — — — — — — — — —

— — — — — — — — — — — — — — — — —

— — — — — — — — — — — — — — — — —

— — — — — — — — — — — — — — — — —

— — — — — — — — — — — — — — — —

But if the story you're telling is not utterly unconventional—if it's not just a bunch of unrelated words strung together—then your story probably consists of *somebody* doing *something . . . somewhere.* Right? Thus, in addition to all the delightfully strange things your imagination can come up with, your *mise en place* should probably include:

- a **hero** (such as a knight or a wizard or a collie)

- a **task** for said hero to perform (in most cases, this task will not be easy; it will entail overcoming obstacles—befriending dragons, fighting inner demons, learning to spell *Azerbaijan*—to achieve a goal)

- and a **world** in which said hero performs said task (also known as the setting of the story)

Those three things are the main elements of most stories. Obvious? Perhaps. But it took me years to learn this simple formula—or maybe, in keeping with the *mise en place* idea, I should say this simple recipe.*

---

*Just to be clear, when I say that you should include those three things in your *mise en place*, I don't mean that you should have an actual hero by your side—although that might help—only the idea for one.

Take my favorite book of all time, *Charlie and the Chocolate Factory*. The hero of the book? Easy. It's Charlie, the poor boy who doesn't have enough to eat. The world of the book? Also easy. Willy Wonka's magical and mysterious chocolate factory—it's right there in the title alongside the name of our hero. Our hero's task? Well, I suppose that one's a little more difficult to discern. In the early part of the book, Charlie's task is to find a golden ticket so as to gain entry to the chocolate factory and earn a lifetime's supply of chocolate. Later, it turns out that he has been unknowingly performing a much larger task: proving his moral worth to Wonka, thereby making himself Wonka's heir and ensuring that he will have not just a lifetime's but an absolutely unlimited supply of chocolate. Thus, you might say, Charlie's real task is to acquire as much chocolate as humanly possible—a task I set for myself every day.

You spoiled the ending!

How can you spoil the best ending of all time? That much chocolate is unspoilable!

Pseudo-intelligence:
To outline or not to outline?

A *mise en place* is not to be confused with that dread thing—I hesitate even to mention the word—an *outline*. If you like outlines—and many do, especially editors and teachers and other people I consider my natural enemies—then great, go to it, outline away. Bullet points. Index cards. Spreadsheets. They're all yours. To me, outlines are worse than unhelpful—they're totally disheartening—for the simple reason that I am never able to complete them. Instead of giving me confidence in the book I'm writing, an outline makes me all too aware of how difficult it's going to be to get to the end. What I like about the idea of the *mise en place* is that it allows you to gather story elements without forcing you to think through your entire novel before it's written. A *mise en place* implies a recipe—but an open-ended one. A recipe that's subject to change.

Now let's get back to your story.

I have already (and very helpfully, I might add!) supplied a task for your hero to perform: finding the missing author—that mysteriously familiar-sounding mystery novelist, I.B. Anonymous. The world of your book is the time and place in which I.B. must be found; and we'll get there soon enough—i.e., at another time and place. Which leaves your hero—him-, her-, or itself—the most important element of a story, according to many writers wiser than I. (Me, I tend to judge books by the number of references to chocolate; you'll notice I try to write the word as often as possible.)

So, my budding young author friend, who is your *protagonist*, as your language arts teacher might put it?

Who is the hero of your book?

CHAPTER THREE

Your Heroes:
From A to Z

I say *heroes*—plural—because, as you no doubt have noted, I've already given you two: the siblings A____ and Z____. Why? With two heroes, there are more opportunities to write dialogue; and, as everyone knows, dialogue is much more fun to read than description. Also, having two heroes allows us to make one a girl and one a boy. That way all your readers will feel represented.

For simplicity's sake, I made A____ and Z____ sister and brother. But you can change most everything about them, including their relationship. Perhaps they're not a girl and a boy after all. Perhaps they're a girl and her pet monster. Or, better yet, a monster and his pet girl.

The one thing you cannot change is the role they play. If they are your heroes, then they are the ones who must track down the missing author. As you create their characters in your imagination,

Ahem, what about rabbits? I don't feel represented.

you should think about what kind of people would be best suited for this role—and what kind least suited. (Sometimes, it's more fun to have an unlikely hero.) From the prologue, we can surmise that A____ and Z____ are curious about their neighbor. Are they reluctant detectives or eager ones? Perhaps they're aspiring authors themselves? You decide.

What matters is that they are actively engaged with their quest and that you, their author, are actively engaged with them.

Pseudo-intelligence:
Is this book a girl book or a boy book?

Few questions irk me more than that one. Memo to parents, children, Santa Claus, and all interested parties: a book does not have a gender. Whether it's pink and sparkly and wearing a tutu, or covered with grass stains and wearing a baseball cap, a book is a book is a book, and anybody can read it, boy, girl, or chimpanzee! And, for the record, my feelings about this question have nothing—absolutely nothing—to do with my own boyhood reading choices. *Little House on the Prairie?* Never heard of it. Nancy Drew? More like Nancy Who? You must have me confused with somebody else. I myself was reading, er, something else. OK, fine, it was *Little Women.* So what...

SIGNATURE PRACTICE

A famous author has to sign her name over and over. True, not every author is going to become famous, but it doesn't hurt to practice. Use this space to perfect your autograph. You will have to learn to write fast if you want to sign hundreds of books at a time, but try not to sacrifice style for speed. A little flourish in that signature, please.

Signature _____

7. SIGNATURE Signature

Failure to sign this claim form may delay processing.

SIGN HERE

Signature

ACKNOWLEDGMENT
I/We have read this disclosure form, and

Signature

SALUTATION SUGGESTIONS

Famously yours,

You're my sister? I'm sorry, I don't remember you.

All it takes is a little luck ... and *a lot* of talent.

What, this old book? I wrote it years ago.

I never forget the little people—
I just don't talk to them anymore.

By the way, I also star in movies.

𝔖𝔦𝔤𝔫𝔞𝔱𝔲𝔯𝔢

Enough dillydallying. It's time for you to get back to work. And I mean it this time!

(See how tough I can be when I want to be? Unfortunately, the toughness never works when I try it on myself.)

Start with your heroes' names. Presumably, A and Z are their initials, but they don't have to be. In fact, I picked the letters to suggest that the names could be anything you like—any names from A to Z. Get it? Just keep in mind that names have power; sometimes a name alone is enough to create a character.

> So if I called you Carrot, would you magically turn into one?

Please enter your heroes' full names here.

A____'s full name: _ _ _ _ _ _ _ _ _ _

Z____'s full name: _ _ _ _ _ _ _ _ _ _

Pseudo-intelligence: The name game

There are as many ways to name a character as there are to name a baby or a newly discovered insect species.

Some authors choose names that express something unique about their character. This might be a color or animal or flower, like Blue or Wolf or Iris. Another author might adopt the name of a favorite pet or the name of a hated PE teacher or the name of a certain teenage singer famous for his dirty-blond bangs. As you may remember, my Secret Series character Max-Ernest has two names because his parents couldn't agree on just one, but there is a secret reason I gave him those two particular names (or pseudonyms, I should say, since his real names are something else entirely). Although he wants desperately to be funny, Max-Ernest can't help being serious—that is, *earnest*. Maximally so. He is earnest to the max. Hence Max-Ernest.*

Other authors think names needn't be so meaningful (or silly); instead, they should be as realistic as possible. Or realistic for the worlds they are portraying. A name that sounds realistic in Maine might not sound realistic on Mars. Isabel Robbins, for example, just doesn't say Martian to me. Izzi, on the other hand, has major Martian potential....

If you have trouble picking a name, do what I do when I'm stuck: choose a book at random—dictionaries are great—open to the middle, and use the first name you find. *Phalanger...? Phalanstery...? Phalanx...?* Let's try again. *Truncheon... Trundle... Trunk...?* Well, you get the idea....

*In the last century there was a real person, an artist, named Max-Ernst, but his art wasn't especially earnest or real; it was *surreal*.

Now that you've named your heroes—if you don't mind, I'll still refer to them as A____ and Z____—I think it would be a good idea to jot down some notes about their personalities and appearance and so on.*

On pages 50–51, you will find a very official-looking character assessment form to fill out. (In reality, there's nothing official about it; I just made it up.) Think of the form as a longer version of one of those irritating little personality quizzes that other kids send around via e-mail. (*You* never send them, I'm sure.) Or else pretend you're choosing attributes for your personal avatar in some virtual world or video game where the goal isn't to win but rather to be as fascinating as possible.

If you get stuck, try answering the questions for yourself; how would you describe *you*? There's no reason you can't model one of your characters on yourself. Or on anybody else you know, for that matter. Just make sure you change enough details to allow for plausible deniability. (*That stubborn, pointy-eared troublemaker? Why on earth would you think I based her on you? Your ears aren't that big.*

---

*According to legend, the Belgian crime writer Georges Simenon wrote dossiers for every one of his characters, dossiers so comprehensive that they included information he never intended to use. Knowing his characters so completely helped him write better, he claimed. Since he published more than two hundred books, I doubt he could have kept track of his characters otherwise.

True, they stick out a bit, but...) You don't want anybody hunting you down in a murderous rage after reading your book.

Trust him on this— he speaks from experience.

Pseudo-intelligence: Is your book autobiographical?

Readers often ask authors if their characters are based on themselves. And almost always, the answer is: yes and no. Sometimes our characters represent the people we wish we were; sometimes they represent the people we fear we might be; and sometimes our characters reveal things about us we never knew. Whatever your intention, my guess is your characters will wind up resembling you in ways you don't expect. Books can be quite scary that way.

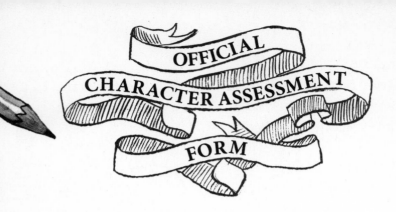

NAME: _

CODE NAME OR PSEUDONYM (a must for any self-respecting character!): _ _ _ _ _ _ _ _ _ _ _ _ _ _ _ _ _

SPECIES (real or invented): _ _ _ _ _ _ _ _ _ _ _ _ _

AGE (in human years unless otherwise specified): _ _ _ _ _ _ _

HAIR COLOR (unless bald…or furry): _ _ _ _ _ _ _ _

EYE COLOR (or colors, if multiple): _ _ _ _ _ _ _ _ _

UNDERWEAR COLOR (You should know your characters from top to bottom!): _ _ _ _ _ _ _ _ _ _ _ _ _ _ _

UNIFORM (cape and tights, shining armor, mascot-style bear suit):
_ _

OTHER DISTINGUISHING PHYSICAL FEATURES
(missing limbs, extra fingers, green skin, a gaseous being with no body):

_ _

PERSONALITY (cautious or impulsive? studious or adventurous? calm or hyperactive? funny or glum?): _ _ _ _ _ _ _ _ _ _ _ _

HOBBIES, INTERESTS, TALENTS (reads minds, charms snakes, swallows swords): _ _ _ _ _ _ _ _ _ _ _ _

EATING HABITS (vegan, eats with mouth open, only eats purple foods): _ _ _ _ _ _ _ _ _ _ _ _ _

PICKS NOSE?   Y/N
(I just threw this one in—you don't have to answer if you're too squeamish.)

CATCHPHRASE (Every hero has to have one!): _ _ _ _ _ _ _

VERBAL TIC (stutters, says *um* and *like* a lot, sing-song voice):
_ _ _ _ _ _ _ _ _ _ _ _ _ _ _ _

THEME SONG: _ _ _ _ _ _ _ _ _ _ _ _ _

SUPERPOWER (and don't say superstrong—that's a cop-out):
_ _ _ _ _ _ _ _ _ _ _ _ _ _ _

GREATEST DESIRE (whether publicly acknowledged or secret):
_ _ _ _ _ _ _ _ _ _ _ _ _ _ _

GREATEST FEAR (clowns, mayonnaise, anything—but choose carefully; this one might come back to bite you, as it were): _ _ _ _ _
_ _ _ _ _ _ _ _ _ _ _ _ _ _ _

FATAL FLAW (pride, greed, jealousy, addiction to a certain type of sweets—your hero's fatal flaw is what will bring him down, and what he will have to overcome before your story is over): _ _ _ _ _ _ _ _

Terrific! Great job! I can see you're an expert, er, *characterizer*! You're on your way to writing a heckuva novel!*

In all seriousness, keep those character profiles handy, not just to help you describe your characters but also to help you plot your story. Your heroes' personalities will help determine the choices they make and thus the course your story takes. Of course, the reverse is also true; you may find your understanding of a character changes as your story progresses. Characters are just like people; no matter how well you think you know them, they always surprise you.

---

*ALL RIGHT, ALL RIGHT, YOU CAUGHT ME. I HAVEN'T ACTUALLY READ ANYTHING YOU'VE WRITTEN. I'M JUST TRYING TO ENCOURAGE YOU IN THAT EMPTY, MEANINGLESS WAY ADULTS SOMETIMES DO. IT'S INSULTING TO YOUR INTELLIGENCE, I KNOW. I APOLOGIZE. I'LL TRY TO BE MORE RESPECTFUL IN THE FUTURE.

Pseudo-assignment:
Voice mail

Now that you know your heroes, write voice mail messages for them. No *Hello, you have reached so-and-so....* Try to be more creative. Are your heroes the type of people to use a song as a greeting? Or are they more likely to greet callers with a recording of a barking dog? Maybe they don't use phones at all but rather communicate through owl or carrier pigeon. Mental telepathy? (What would telepathic voice mail sound like?) Don't forget to include a few voice mail messages or texts that your heroes are likely to receive in return. Who are your heroes' friends? What kinds of things are going on in your heroes' lives that might appear in phone messages? For extra credit, record one of your heroes' fictional greetings on your own voice mail and confuse all the real people who call you.

RANDOM WRITING TIP: BRAINSTORMS

Never let yourself get caught unprepared in a brainstorm.

Many writers will tell you always to carry a notepad and pen so that you can jot down any and all ideas that happen to fall from the sky. Myself, I only carry a pen. I find that the palm of my hand is a much better writing surface than a notepad when it's raining.

CHAPTER FOUR

AKA Chapter 1

So, my dear author, getting back to your book, how do you think you should begin your first chapter? The next day seems like the most natural place to start, does it not?

Unless you have a better idea, you should probably begin with A____ and/or Z____ waking up.

Use this moment to establish the personalities that you so carefully analyzed earlier. What do their bedrooms look like? Do they jump out of bed or linger under the covers? Do they pick up rumpled clothes from the floor or take a neatly folded shirt out of a drawer? How do they brush their teeth? Or don't they? Do they have any funny or weird morning rituals they wouldn't want anybody to see? Remember, you want your reader to love your heroes enough to spend an entire book with them—but that doesn't mean your reader has to *like* everything about them.

WRITE THIS:

Describe A_____ or Z_____ or both as they wake up in the morning. As you write, to maintain dramatic tension, make reference to the frightening sounds Z_____ heard the previous night.* Do A_____ and Z_____ wake up thinking about all the horrible things that might have happened? If you need more space, attach an extra page. Or just write over my words. I don't need them. And don't forget to title your chapter—whether at the beginning or the end.**

*WHAT IS *DRAMATIC TENSION*? DRAMATIC TENSION IS WHAT INCREASES AS YOU WAIT FOR A DEFINITION OF DRAMATIC TENSION. IT IS WHAT KEEPS YOU READING. IT IS KNOWING THAT A SURPRISE AWAITS BEHIND THE NEXT CORNER. DRAMATIC TENSION IS WAITING FOR THE AX TO FALL...AND BELIEVE ME, IT WILL.

**I ALWAYS NAME MY CHAPTERS AT THE END; I USED TO NAME CHAPTERS BEFORE WRITING THEM, BUT YOU WOULDN'T BELIEVE HOW MANY CHAPTERS I'VE CALLED "ADVENTURE DOWN AT THE QUARRY" ONLY TO FIND THAT THERE IS NO QUARRY.

The Case of the Missing Author
Chapter 1

- - - - - - - - - - - - - - - - - - -

- - - - - - - - - - - - - - - - - - -

In which A_____ and Z_____ wake up and demonstrate winning character traits that make your reader want to read a whole book about them.

- - - - - - - - - - - - - - - - - - - -

- - - - - - - - - - - - - - - - - - - -

- - - - - - - - - - - - - - - - - - - -

- - - - - - - - - - - - - - - - - - - -

- - - - - - - - - - - - - - - - - - - -

- - - - - - - - - - - - - - - - - - - -

- - - - - - - - - - - - - - - - - - - -

- - - - - - - - - - - - - - - - - - - -

- - - - - - - - - - - - - - - - - - - -

- - - - - - - - - - - - - - - - - - - -

Good. Now we know that your heroes didn't die overnight—always an important fact to establish. But did *their neighbor* die overnight? That's the question your readers will be—

Oh, no. I just had a terrible thought. Before we get to all that fun mystery stuff inside I.B.'s house, we have some ugly writing business to attend to:

PARENTS!!!!!!!!!!!!!!!!!!!!!!!!*

There's no way around it: they have to be part of this chapter.

You know what they say: *Parents—can't live with 'em, can't live without 'em.* Parents, as any writer of books for young people will tell you, are the worst. They're always getting in the way, making your heroes eat breakfast or do their homework or wash dishes—anything to keep them from going off on an adventure. Parents can stop a good book in its tracks. In that sense, a book is much like life.

The difference is: in a book you can dispatch your parents however you please. Writing is very convenient that way.

Have you ever noticed how many orphans there are in children's books and movies? *Oliver Twist. Anne of Green Gables. James and the Giant Peach.*

---

*STYLE NOTE: NEVER OVERUSE EXCLAMATION MARKS; IT IS THE MARK OF AN AMATEUR WRITER. YOUR WORDS SHOULD BE ASSERTIVE ENOUGH TO STAND ALONE. THEN AGAIN, I MUST ADMIT, EXCLAMATION MARKS CAN BE FUN!!!!!!! !!!!!!!!!!!!!!!!!!!!!!!!!!!!!

Harry Potter. The list, as they say, goes on. That's not because we authors have some deep desire to kill off our parents; it's because we're trying to remove them from the action, and death is the most expedient way.*

So, how do you want to get rid of *your* parents? Sorry, I mean, *your heroes'* parents. (I'm sure you want to keep any real parent you happen to have!) If they're not home when A_____ and Z_____ wake up, your reader needs to know why.

CHECK ALL THOSE THAT APPLY:

☐   They died in their sleep.

☐   They were buried in an avalanche.

☐   They fell through a wormhole.

☐   They were lost at sea.

☐   They're currently floating in outer space.

☐   They're trapped in a parallel universe.

---

*FOR A LONGER LIST OF LITERARY ORPHANS, TURN TO THE PARENTAL OBITUARY SECTION IN THE APPENDIX.

☐ They're geologists who work year-round in a subterranean laboratory studying the earth's fiery-hot core.

☐ Actually, they are alive and well. It's just that they are oblivious, head-in-the-clouds types. They don't notice when the toast is burning, let alone a child.

☐ Other, more peculiar reason for parents' nonappearance:

— — — — — — — — — — — — — — — —

(One thing we know for sure: your heroes' parents are not good responsible healthy living parents who are very concerned with their kids' welfare. *That* would never work in a book.)

Phew. Now that's taken care of.

Bye, Mom!

Bye, Dad!

Pseudo-intelligence: Beware a bad back!

Once you've picked your preferred method of parental execution, how do you impart that gruesome information—or *backstory*, as we call it in the writing trade—to your reader? Any number of ways. A_____ and Z_____ could bring up the memory of a parent in dialogue. There could be photos of their parents in their bedrooms or in the kitchen. A_____ or Z_____ could have a morbid fear of whatever it was that killed their parents. (Perhaps their parents choked on peanut butter, and A_____ and Z_____ have never been able to hear the words *peanut butter*, much less eat the dread spread since?) Or you could simply tell your reader what happened; sometimes the direct approach is best. One word of warning: backstory is very boring if it's not written properly. A bad backstory can stab your story right in the back. My advice: write your backstory like your front story—i.e., like it's taking place in the present. When in doubt, erase your backstory altogether— even if it means leaving your book as backless as a hospital gown. On second thought...

PROCRASTINATION PAGE

OPEN REFRIGERATOR.

FIND NOTHING THAT YOU WANT TO EAT.

CLOSE REFRIGERATOR.

REPEAT.

(Remember, we writers are working *all the time*, no matter what it may seem like we're doing.)

CHAPTER FIVE

Location:
The Author's House

Let's get back to the question of what happened the night before. What exactly did Z____ hear? *Who laughed? Who cried? What made that thud?* Yes, it could turn out that he imagined the whole thing, but I'd prefer that we come up with a better explanation. I don't know about you, but I've always hated the old it-was-all-just-a-dream scenario.

Since I'm in such a good mood, I'll start the second chapter for you. (It must be the way you got rid of your parents so handily—I mean *your heroes' parents, your heroes' parents!*) If I miss a few words here or there, please fill in the blanks.

The Case of the Missing Author
Chapter 2

- - - - - - - - - - - - - - - - -

- - - - - - - - - - - - - - - -

In which A____ and Z____ wonder about what happened in the author's house the night before.

With their parents gone, it was A____'s respon-sibility to bring in the newspaper and the mail. After finishing her

- ☐ whole-grain cereal
- ☐ sausage-and-pancakes breakfast pockets
- ☐ cold leftover pizza
- ☐ homework
- ☐ farm chores
- ☐ morning calisthenics
- ☐ game of pinochle

she stepped out onto their front porch.

The house across the street was quiet. She shivered, looking at it. Had she been too quick to dismiss her brother's concerns the night before, she wondered. What if something ter-rible had happened to their neighbor?

Pushing away her grim thoughts, she opened the mailbox; on top of a pile of junk mail was a bulging manila envelope. When she saw the name on the envelope, she wrinkled her face in confusion. Why on earth would an envelope addressed to *him* land in *their* mailbox? She looked at the address under the name—and (gasped) in surprise.

INSERT CATCH-PHRASE (SEE CHARACTER PROFILE)

" — — — — — — — — — — — — — — — !"

So *that* was who was living across the street!

Shivered? Gasped? Talk about overused words, Mr. Master Writer!

That's why I circled them—so the reader would replace them with better ones!

"It could be a joke," said Z____ a moment later. " — — — — — — — — — — — — , maybe somebody just calls him that because he's so secretive or something."

"Did you look at the return address? It's from his publishers—Little Clown."

I'm the one who circled them.

INSERT VERBAL TIC (SEE CHARACTER PROFILE*)

***HENCEFORTH, I WILL NOT CUE YOUR CHARACTERS' CATCH-PHRASES OR VERBAL TICS. PLEASE INSERT THEM WHEREVER YOU SEE FIT.**

Oh.

Z____ stared at the envelope on the table. It just didn't seem possible that their mystery neighbor was actually I.B. Anonymous, his favorite author in the—

Oh, really? His favorite?

Why not? Fine, we'll let the reader choose—

It just didn't seem possible that their mystery neighbor was actually I.B. Anonymous, his

☐ favorite
☐ least favorite

author in the world.

"I thought he was living in the jungle or Greenland or someplace," Z____ muttered.

"Yeah, and he also says he has a talking rabbit assistant who types his books for him!" said his sister. "That's all pretend. Duh."

"You don't know anything about him," said Z____.

I'll tell you what's pretend—the idea that you write your books yourself!

"I'm the one who gave you his books!"

Z____ turned over the envelope. "We have to open this. That's the only way to know for sure it's him."

A____ looked at her brother, aghast.

Just keep typing.

"It came to our house, didn't it? Besides, look at the way it's taped. We can tape it right back up. He'll never know," said Z____. "C'mon, admit it, you're curious."

"That doesn't matter; it's not ours. That's like...stealing."

"Never mind, you're right; we should just put it in his mailbox."

"Well, we don't have to put it in his mailbox," said his sister slyly. "We could knock on the door. That's what most people would do, isn't it?"

Z____ grinned. "Yeah, you're right, it's more polite. And if we accidentally see inside his house, well, that's not our fault....Besides," he added, his expression growing serious, "we should probably make sure he's OK."

A____ nodded. That was what she'd been thinking.

Now, if this were *my* book, I might try to draw out the suspense at this point. Rather than letting them immediately knock on I.B.'s door, for example, I might throw in some more background information about A____ or Z____. Or I might have somebody call on the phone to say one of them had won a big prize or that their school had burned down or that they had missed a piano lesson.

Or I might just linger on the description of I.B.'s house as A____ and Z____ slowly walk toward it. Like this:

From the outside, I.B. Anonymous's house looked—

What am I doing? You're the writer. What does I.B.'s house look like? *You* tell *me*.

Think about it: he's a secretive author. He wouldn't want his house to call too much attention to itself. For that reason, the house might look like every other house on the block. Anonymous, in other words, like I.B. himself. But what if his house is the only house on his side of the street; how could he make his house blend in then? Is it camouflaged? Protected with an invisibility shield?*

Perhaps there's something else about I.B. you want to convey in your description. His eccentricity, for example. (Maybe the house is painted royal blue? The front door is on the roof? The house is upside down?) Or his absentmindedness. (The yard is overgrown? He parks his car in the living room?) Or his paranoia. (Maybe there are telescopes on the roof? Bulletproof glass? Multiple alarm systems?)

*IF YOU THINK I MIGHT HAVE OTHER REASONS FOR NOT DESCRIBING THE AUTHOR'S HOUSE—IF YOU THINK I MIGHT BE AFRAID OF GIVING TOO MUCH AWAY, LIKE MY OWN LOCATION—THEN YOU ARE AS PARANOID AS I AM. AND YOU ARE 100 PERCENT CORRECT.

Pseudo-assignment: Instructions

Invent a strange new device—something you might find on an alien planet, for instance. Write instructions for using the device without ever giving away exactly what the device is used for. Alternatively, think of a very familiar item—for example, a peanut butter and jelly sandwich—and write operating instructions for an alien to read. (Remember, the alien may never have eaten anything before, let alone a sandwich.) Show instructions to your friends and make them guess what the instructions refer to. If you have no friends, then give the instructions straight to an alien.

What about his stinginess with his employees? You know, like the fact that there are no carrots anywhere in the house?

Quiet, rabbit!

WRITE THIS:

In the space below, please describe I.B.'s house. Draw it, too. Even if your drawing isn't very good (my drawings never are), it might help you visualize what you're writing about.

The Case of the Missing Author
Chapter 2 (cont.)

In which I.B.'s house is first described.

— — — — — — — — — — — — — — —

— — — — — — — — — — — — — — —

— — — — — — — — — — — — — — —

— — — — — — — — — — — — — — —

— — — — — — — — — — — — — — —

— — — — — — — — — — — — — — —

— — — — — — — — — — — — — — —

— — — — — — — — — — — — — — —

COMPLETE
THE DRAWING

Do you feel like you got I.B.'s house right? (I certainly hope you didn't—I, I mean, *he* has enough trouble staying hidden as it is!) In any event, let's move on. Your reader has waited long enough. It's time to look inside.

Z_ _ _ _ knocked on the door, his heart racing. There was no response from inside. But as he knocked a second time, the door opened _____ly.* A_ _ _ _ and Z_ _ _ _ held their breath, waiting to see who opened the door—I.B. or his murderer or some other, unknown force.

If you think the door opened by magic—whether by mechanical illusion or real magic—you can add a sentence here saying so. Of course, the other possibility is that the door wasn't completely closed and the force of Z_ _ _ _'s knock opened it.

"Hello?"
When nobody answered, they stepped inside.

---

*CREAKILY? NOISELESSLY? THIS SEEMS LIKE A GOOD SPOT FOR SPOOKY WRITING (OR FOR WRITING *SPOOKILY*). SPEAKING OF SPOOKING, YOU SHOULD KNOW THAT SOME WRITERS ARE SPOOKED BY ADVERBS. THEY THINK -*LY* WORDS ARE UNNECESSARY AND SLOW YOUR WRITING DOWN. I SUFFER FROM NO SUCH SCRUPLES AND CHEERFULLY—NO, HAPPILY; NO, JOYFULLY; NO, EXUBERANTLY!— EXULT IN USING ADVERBS EXCESSIVELY.

Pseudo-assignment:
Snoop training

No, I do not recommend that you walk into your neighbor's house and snoop around uninvited (although I admit it might prove inspiring for a budding writer's imagination). As an alternative, try snooping around your own home, pretending you're a first-time visitor. What things stand out? What can you conclude about the people who live there? Write a list of observations and hypotheses based strictly on what you see, not on what you already know. And if your brother gets mad at you for looking in his closet, tell him you had no choice; P.B. made you do it. It's all part of your training as a writer.

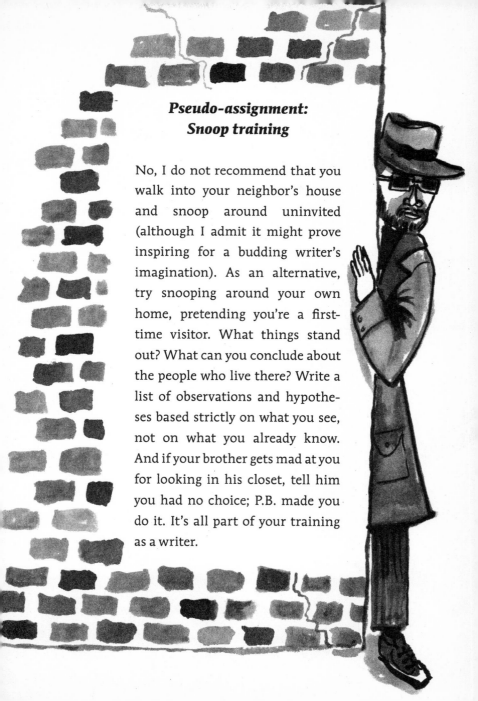

CHAPTER SIX

Location (Continued): On the Inside

INSERT CHAPTER TITLE HERE

The Case of the Missing Author
Chapter 3

- - - - - - - - - - - - - - - - - - -

- - - - - - - - - - - - - - - - - - -

Having read all of I.B.'s books, A____ and Z____ had been expecting the inside of I.B.'s house to look like a _____, but instead it looked like a _____.

Nothing suggested that a tragedy had occurred the night before. More than a few _____ brand chocolate bar wrappers littered the floor,

but they looked as if I.B. had just dropped them there, not like they'd fallen in a fight.*

"What a slob!" whispered A____.

Well, at least that part is true!

That's not the point. I'm trying to show them how a writer lays clues....

Aside from the _____ brand chocolate bar wrappers, the one thing Z____ recognized from I.B.'s books was an old, fraying black top hat, perched on top of a bureau.

Clues that you never clean up?

"Hey, it's Italo's hat! Or it's just how he described Italo's hat, anyway."

---

*I'M SORRY, YOU WILL HAVE TO SUPPLY A BRAND NAME YOURSELF. THE ACTUAL BRAND OF CHOCOLATE BAR I EAT—ER, THAT I.B. EATS—IS STRICTLY CONFIDENTIAL. IN THE WRONG HANDS, THIS INFORMATION COULD BE MY DOWNFALL.

If his books were to be believed, I.B. had inherited his top hat from the old magician Italo Barbero, leader of the secret organization known as the Cester Society.

In his Series of Secrets, I.B. wrote about himself in the character of middle school student Jon-Thomas, an aspiring magician (as well as aspiring comedian). Together with his best friend, Tess, Jon-Thomas joins the Cester Society and comes to think of Italo as a sort of father figure. At the end of I.B.'s series, Italo disappears, leaving only his hat for his young friends to find—a conclusion both Z____ and A____ had found frustrating, to say the least.

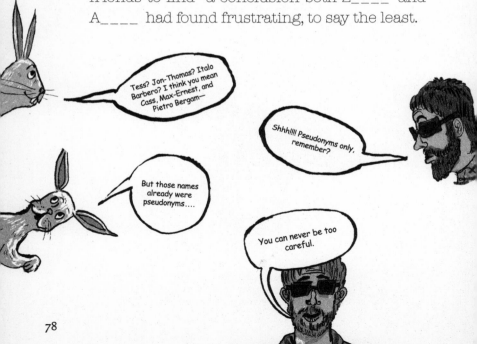

Tess? Jon-Thomas? Italo Barbero? I think you mean Cass, Max-Ernest, and Pietro Bergam—

Shhh!!!! Pseudonyms only, remember?

But those names already were pseudonyms....

You can never be too careful.

Z____ placed the manila envelope on the bureau and glanced inside the top hat, half-expecting to find a rabbit, but the hat was empty.

Under the couch, I.B.'s gray cat
☐ Tiger
☐ Snowball
☐ Boots
☐ Muffin
☐ Cocoa
☐ Cacao
☐ (Other) _____

crouched, his hair bristling on his back. When A____ reached to pet him, the cat slunk out of sight.

Strange, A____ thought; when she'd met him on the street, the cat hadn't been especially affectionate—how many cats are?—but at least he had permitted her to touch him.

"When did he get so scared of me?" she whispered to her brother.

Z replied:

a. "What am I, psychic?"

b. "Have you looked in the mirror lately?"

c. "I don't know, it's kinda weird."

d. "Maybe he figured out you're part dog."

e. "_____."

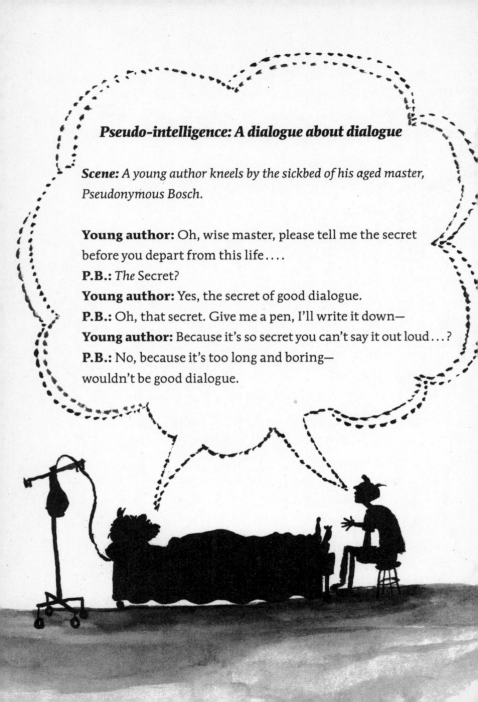

Pseudo-intelligence: A dialogue about dialogue

Scene: *A young author kneels by the sickbed of his aged master, Pseudonymous Bosch.*

Young author: Oh, wise master, please tell me the secret before you depart from this life....
P.B.: *The* Secret?
Young author: Yes, the secret of good dialogue.
P.B.: Oh, that secret. Give me a pen, I'll write it down—
Young author: Because it's so secret you can't say it out loud...?
P.B.: No, because it's too long and boring—
wouldn't be good dialogue.

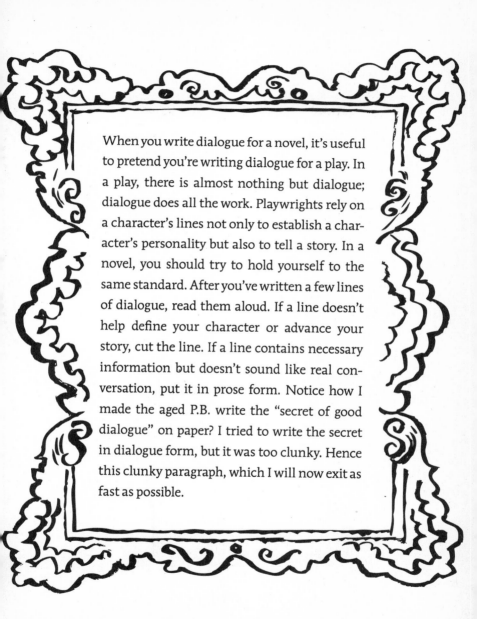

When you write dialogue for a novel, it's useful to pretend you're writing dialogue for a play. In a play, there is almost nothing but dialogue; dialogue does all the work. Playwrights rely on a character's lines not only to establish a character's personality but also to tell a story. In a novel, you should try to hold yourself to the same standard. After you've written a few lines of dialogue, read them aloud. If a line doesn't help define your character or advance your story, cut the line. If a line contains necessary information but doesn't sound like real conversation, put it in prose form. Notice how I made the aged P.B. write the "secret of good dialogue" on paper? I tried to write the secret in dialogue form, but it was too clunky. Hence this clunky paragraph, which I will now exit as fast as possible.

Cautiously, they began to explore the rest of the house, starting with the kitchen.

"If he knew he was going away, he could have at least done the dishes," said A_ _ _ _, looking at the sink.

"He wouldn't have known he was going away if he was kidnapped by the Evening Sun," said Z_ _ _ _ darkly, referring to the villainous organization that haunted the Cester Society throughout I.B.'s Series of Secrets.

"The Evening Sun? First of all, I keep telling you, his books are just books. They're not real," said A_ _ _ _. "Second of all, I don't see any white gloves lying around, do you?"

"Exactly. They never take off their gloves."

"So you're saying the fact that they didn't leave gloves proves that they were here? That makes no sense."

There was an open doorway at the end of the hall. I.B.'s office. They were drawn to it like _____ to a _____.

Most of the room was piled high with more _____ brand chocolate bar wrappers and half-eaten pieces of _____. But, curiously, the middle of the room was empty. It was as if some centrifugal force had spun all of I.B.'s belongings away. Except for a single leather notebook that lay on the floor in the exact center of the room.

A handwritten note was clipped to the notebook. "Look—it's for us!" cried Z____, holding up the note to show his sister. "How did he know we were going to be here?"

Dear A____ and Z____,

Welcome! I've been inspecting you.
Here's my new book for you to expect.

By the way, can you feed the cat?
I may be gone awhile. . . .

Secretly, I.B.

A____ frowned. "*Expect?* I think he flipped the words. He must have meant *inspect*—you know, like, *I've been expecting you. Here's my new book to inspect.*"

"You're missing the point—it's his new book and it's not even published yet! You know how many kids would kill to get their hands on this?!"

"Well, I hope they wouldn't kill *him*—"

"I didn't mean it that way."

Z____ eagerly opened the notebook, but as soon as he started flipping through the pages, his face fell.

"What—what's wrong?" asked A____.

Z____ turned the pages toward his sister. The notebook was blank. "Why did he leave it for us if it's not even written?"

A____ shrugged. "I guess he meant *expect* after all. There's no book yet to inspect."

"Maybe it's written in invisible ink?"

Z____ performed a few quick tests, but he couldn't find evidence of any hidden writing anywhere in the notebook.*

He was about to toss the notebook aside when A____ pointed to a page near the front. "Hey, what's that say?"

There were four names written faintly on it—not in invisible ink, just old-fashioned number two pencil.

---

*IF A PIECE OF PAPER HAS BEEN WRITTEN ON WITH LEMON JUICE—ONE OF THE MOST COMMON TYPES OF INVISIBLE INK—HEATING THE PAPER WILL REVEAL THE HIDDEN WRITING. JUST DON'T LET THE TEMPERATURE OF YOUR PAPER RISE ABOVE 451 DEGREES FAHRENHEIT. THAT IS THE TEMPERATURE AT WHICH PAPER STARTS TO BURN, DESTROYING NOT JUST INVISIBLE INK BUT VISIBLE INK AS WELL.

Horatio

Eleanor

Leopold

Penelope

"Do you think he was trying to pick names for his characters?" asked A_____.

"No, look at the first initials," said Z_____, growing excited again. "It's code, just like in his first book! ***H - E - L - P. HELP.***"

"Wait, you think that's a message for us?" asked A_____.

A_____ and Z_____ looked at each other.

I.B. was in trouble. He wanted their help.

I'm sure you're familiar with the term *cliffhanger*, even if you've never hung off a cliff yourself. It refers to a single drip of mucus that is hanging precipitously from a nostril, refusing to drop to the ground. It also refers to a moment in a story, usually a dramatic and exciting moment, when the story's author stops the action in order to prolong suspense.

Whenever possible, it is wise to end a chapter on a cliffhanger. It keeps your reader hungry for more. (For more story, not more mucus—don't be disgusting!) I advise just such a chapter break now.

PROCRASTINATION PAGE

DEVELOP AN ITCH
ON A HARD-TO-REACH SPOT
ON YOUR BACK.

GO SLOWLY CRAZY
TRYING TO SCRATCH IT.

CHAPTER SEVEN

Plot...Plot...Plot

Help!

No, really, I mean it—**HELP!** I can't get this chocolate bar unwrapped—my fingernails are too short. Oh, there we go...never mind... *hmmghf*...not bad...

Now, where was I? Oh, yes—help. A plea for help often represents a turning point in a story, or more precisely *a point of no return*. Heroes who refuse the plea live to regret the choice, forever haunted by the repercussions of their cowardice. Heroes who respond to the plea find themselves caught in treacherous situations, seemingly with no way out.

> In other words, if you hear somebody cry for help, you should...cry for help.

On that optimistic note, how are your heroes going to react to the plea in I.B.'s notebook? That is to say, how are *you* going to react as the author of *The Case of the Missing Author*?

Sure, the answer might be: your heroes ignore the plea and go home. But that wouldn't make for a very dramatic story, would it? (Unless, perhaps, you were planning on having them murdered that night in their sleep? A double murder would be very dramatic indeed.) Let's assume, for the sake of argument, that A_____ and Z_____ are good-hearted young people who are distressed by I.B.'s message. They may also feel some guilt about not having tried to help the imperiled author the night before. For whatever reason, they want to help him now.

So, my dear reader-turned-writer, what do they do to help I.B.? **What happens next?**

Take it from me, helping an author is always a mistake!

Well...?

I'm waiting.

Tap...tap...tap...

I'm sorry, I fell asleep.
What did you say?

Now *you* want help? If you're unwrapping a chocolate bar, I would be glad to assist. I know I said my nails were short, but that's only a minor—

Oh, you mean help with your book. Again? This is getting ridiculous. I'm beginning to think it might have been easier to write this book myself!

What can I do that will enable me to wash my hands of *The Case of the Missing Author* once and for all?

Let me think. From what I can tell, what you need the most help with is...

PLOT

Plot...plot...plot...

Hear that?

It is the sound of ink dropping from a pen as a writer struggles to come up with a— you know what comes next— plot.

Few words are scarier to a writer than the *p*-word. (Is it an accident that a square of earth where a dead author is buried is called a *plot*? I think not.*) And yet, like many scary things—monsters under the bed, ghosts in the closet, politicians on TV—plot turns out not to have much substance when you look at it up close.

See—

PLOT

Oh, who am I kidding? The only thing that scares me as much as plot is an outline—which makes an outline of the word *plot* (see above) the scariest thing of all!

Put simply, plot is structure. Plot is beginning, middle, and end—and how you get from one to the other to the other. Plot is *what happens next*. Plot is the hardest part.

What are the rules for plotting a novel?

I am tempted to answer that there are none. As a rule, I'm against rules about writing. But I am also against boring writing. Without a good plot your story will not only be shapeless, it will be dull.

---

*PERHAPS THE DOUBLE MEANING OF *PLOT* IS THE REASON THAT AUTHORS' BURIAL PLOTS ARE SUCH POPULAR TOURIST ATTRACTIONS. REPUTEDLY, SO MANY VISITORS KISSED THE TOMBSTONE OF THE NINETEENTH-CENTURY PLAY-WRIGHT AND POET OSCAR WILDE THAT THE FRENCH CEMETERY WHERE HE WAS BURIED, PÈRE LACHAISE, HAD TO DISALLOW IT.

Authors and critics of various stripes have tried for centuries to boil down the elements of a good plot. Some people break up stories into three or four or more "acts" (as in a play). Others describe the five "stages" of a plot or the eight "points" that make a story arc. To convey their theories, they present plot diagrams and timelines. Plot pyramids. Even plot snowflakes (really!).

My contribution to this plot stew follows. Think of it as a more elaborate *mise en place* than I offered earlier. A *mise en plot*, perhaps? No, forget the cooking metaphors. Let's switch to something more destination-oriented: *a plot map*. Directions for that crazy road trip you're taking your reader on. A book, after all, should be like a family vacation, with plenty of sightseeing, together time, and rest—in other words, flat tires, fighting, and unmitigated disaster.

PLOT MAP

TRIP PREVIEW: TEASER

1

Ride the roaring rapids!
Look inside the mouth of a crocodile!
See a ten-foot-tall ball of yarn!
A glossy brochure advertising the
incredible trip ahead...

Fool's Gold CASINO

ROUTE 66

VISIT

BACK HOME: THE DENOUEMENT

7

There's no place like home. Or is there?
By the time you go to bed, you're already
feeling antsy. When's the next trip?

PACKING UP: INTRODUCTION OF CHARACTERS AND WORLD

2

When you get to see all your
belongings in piles on the floor.
Don't forget to bring clean
underwear!

MOM DAD SIS DOG

DEPARTURE: INCITING INCIDENT

3

What? They discovered gold in the
Grand Canyon after all these years!
Let's go—now!

HOME

THE ROAD HOME

6

So your car was smashed and the only gold you found was the fool's kind. At least you got to see the Grand Canyon—the bottom of it. And now you get to walk hundreds of miles back home! What a lesson you've learned. (Wait—what was the lesson again?)

Falling Rock

DESTINATION REACHED: THE CLIMAX

Grand Canyon 5

Hooray, you finally reached the Grand Canyon! Only it's so foggy that you can't see anything, and your father is about to drive over the edge. Can you stop the car even though you're afraid of heights and you've only just discovered your superpowers...?

GAS

GETTING THERE IS HALF THE FUN: THE QUEST

4

MOTEL

The main part of your road trip—when everything that can go wrong does. Flat tire...broken cell phone...parents threatening divorce...lost baby brother...Bad luck? Are you kidding? This is the stuff that stories are made of. As writers, we call it "conflict."

Well, there you have it: a map to help you plot the course of your writing journey.

Personally, I have a lot of trouble reading maps. As for directions, I'm one of those infuriating people who refuse, on principle, to ask for them. As a result, I rarely get anywhere. You undoubtedly are much more sensible than I am, and have a much better sense of direction. With any luck, my plot map will lead you straight to your story—plus or minus a few detours, of course.

In a sense, plot is the discovery of story. Or the story of the discovery of story.

And what do you call a story about discovering a story? The same thing you call a plot about uncovering a plot.

A mystery.

Which takes us right back to *The Case of the Missing Author.*

CHAPTER EIGHT

Mysteries: Gumshoes

Now you have officially departed on your authorial road trip. Your inciting incident is in place: the author is missing and he needs your heroes' help. It's time for their quest to begin in earnest. It's time for them to set about finding him.

In a classic mystery, a *whodunit*, a detective has to identify the villain. In other words, he has to figure out who has committed a crime. Which involves figuring out when, where, how, and why the crime was committed. Which is to say, a detective's job is to figure out the story of the crime.

How does he do this? He reads the evidence, of course.

Your book is no different.

In order to find I.B., your heroes will have to play detective, which means examining evidence, looking for clues, and coming to some sort of hypothesis about what happened. (It can also mean donning a trench coat, sunglasses, and fedora, then knocking on strangers' doors and demanding a handout—but that's Halloween, this is a book.)

Put yourself in their shoes. Or perhaps I should say in their *gumshoes*.* What is the first step A_____ and Z_____ would take after the initial shock of seeing the help message? What evidence would they try to read?

Would they dig around I.B.'s yard for a buried body? Listen to his phone messages? Interrogate his cat?

My guess is that the evidence A_____ and Z_____ would first try to read is the most readable evidence at hand: I.B.'s mail. Remember the manila envelope, the one from I.B.'s publishers that landed seemingly by accident in their mailbox? Now they have an excuse to open it, do they not? I.B.'s life may be at stake, Z_____ would likely say. This is no time to worry about the morality of opening somebody else's mail.

Well, what would *you* say? More to the point, what would you *write*? If you think opening I.B.'s mail is so morally reprehensible that you can't

Yes, would you, please? I hate that cat!

---

*A DETECTIVE IS SOMETIMES KNOWN AS A "GUMSHOE." (THIS IS EITHER BECAUSE DETECTIVES WALK SO MUCH OR BECAUSE THE SOLES OF THEIR SHOES MUST BE SOFT TO BE SILENT—I'M NOT SURE WHICH.) ALL AUTHORS PUT THEMSELVES IN A GUMSHOE'S SHOES AT ONE TIME OR ANOTHER; RE-CREATING PAST EVENTS (REAL OR IMAGINED) IS THE JOB OF DETECTIVE AND WRITER ALIKE.

Pseudo-assignment: Get a clue

Knowing how and where to lay clues is a key skill for any mystery writer (and also for criminals who want to throw their pursuers off the scent). Prove your mystery-writing mettle by matching the clue to the crime:

CLUE:	CRIME:
POWDERED-SUGAR MUSTACHE	BORING WRITING
BROWN FINGERPRINTS	POOR ORAL HYGIENE
UNREAD BOOK LYING ON THE FLOOR	STOLEN CHOCOLATE BAR
BROWN TEETH	MISSING DOUGHNUT

imagine your characters doing it no matter what the circumstances, then I commend you—but you're the wrong person to write this book.* Put this book down now and go write something else. If, on the other hand, you're dying to know what's inside the envelope, turn the page:

*Naturally, I'm not suggesting that you should go through *your* neighbor's mail. But anybody who claims (like I.B.) that he lives in the jungle and communicates through penguins is fair game.

The Case of the Missing Author
Chapter 4

- - - - - - - - - - - - - - - - - - -

- - - - - - - - - - - - - - - - - - -

In which A____ and Z____ pore through their neighbor's private mail.

Z____ dumped the contents of the envelope unceremoniously onto the floor.

It was fan mail—if you could call a barrage of questions, demands, and conspiracy theories fan mail. Many of the letters adopted I.B.'s notoriously "snarky" tone.* Some were downright hostile.

Dear I.B.,

What is your real name? If you tell me, I'll give you a hundred pounds of chocolate. If you don't tell me, I'll send you a hundred jars of mayonnaise.

Signed,
I won't tell if you won't

---

*I'M SORRY—I HAD TO PUT *SNARKY* IN SCARE QUOTES. I DON'T LIKE THE WORD IN GENERAL, AND I CERTAINLY DON'T LIKE IT APPLIED TO ME—ER, I MEAN, TO I.B. I PREFER TO DESCRIBE MY WRITING WITH WORDS LIKE *IRONIC...SOPHISTICATED...SUBTLE...ERUDITE....*SHALL I GO ON?

I.B.:

What is the Secret?

I won't tell anyone with white gloves, I swear.

—Fingers crossed

I.B.: IF YOU DON'T WANT ANYBODY TO READ YOUR BOOKS, WHY DO YOU WRITE THEM? THAT DOESN'T MAKE ANY SENSE.

—CONFUSED READER

I.B.—Is the Cester Society real? How do I join?

P.S.—I figured out why it's called Cester—it's an anagram for Secret. See, now you have to let me in!

Dear Mr. Anonymous,

I have to write a book report on your book, but I can't find any information about you, and the report is due tomorrow!

Please, can you just answer these questions:

Are you a man or a woman? Where were you born?

Do you have any pets? What is your book about?

What is your favorite color?

Please write back soon!!!

I mean it!!!

101

Dear I.B.-Is it just a coincidence
that you have the same initials
as the magician Italo Barbero,
or are you the same person?
Sincerely,
Xxxxxxx
(See, two can play at that game!)

I.B., I know who you
are...JON-Thomas!
Evidence: You both
like chocolate. You
both like puzzles.
And you both can't
keep a secret! If
you don't write
back, I'm going to
tell everyone!

Dear I.B.-The Evening Sun
is watching you. Mwahaha.

Evilly yours,
Madame Mal and Doctor Y

P.S. -Just kidding. I'm not really
part of the Evening Sun. Or am I...?
Cue scary music
Dun da da dun...dun...

I.B.-
I want to
be a writer.
What advice
do you have?

Dear I.B.:
I HAVE TO KNOW THE SECRET!
WHAT IS THE SECRET?
TELL ME THE SECRET!!!!!

Dude, I hate
to tell you,
but I caught
a typo in your
third book. Too
late to fix it.
Just thought
you should
know. Later.

DEAR IB: I JUST FINISHED YOUR LAST BOOK AND I CAN'T BELIEVE YOU LEFT US HANGING LIKE THAT! WHAT IS THE SECRET?! WHERE DID ITALO GO?!! WHAT HAPPENED TO TESS AND JON-THOMAS?!!! ARE YOU STILL FRIENDS WITH TESS??!!! SERIOUSLY, PLEASE PLEASE WRITE MORE. I'M BEGGING YOU. *HOLDS CHOCOLATE IN FRONT OF NOSE*

SINCERELY,
YOUR DEVASTATED AND FORLORN READER

Dear I.B.,
These are the things I hate the most about your books:

– – – – – – – – – – –

– – – – – – – – – – –

– – – – – – – – – – –

– – – – – – – – – – –

– – – – – – – – – – –

– – – – – – – – – – –

– – – – – – – – – – –

– – – – – – – – – – –

WRITE YOUR OWN LETTER HERE

One letter stuck out because it wasn't handwritten or typed like the others; it was composed with letters and pictures cut out of magazines and newspapers. It looked like a ransom note or a flyer for a rock band.

Hmm. Ominous letter, is it not? As detectives, A_____ and Z_____ could hardly avoid asking some scary questions about it.

Their thinking might go something like this:

The Case of the Missing Author
Chapter 4 (cont.)

"See this? It's like a picture code," said Z____, holding the last letter. "That's X-fan, like ex-fan of I.B.'s books. Like he used to be a fan, but he isn't anymore."

"Yeah, I get it," said A____, looking over her brother's shoulder. "It's not that subtle."

"He sounds pretty mad."

"If it's a he. Could be a she," A____ pointed out. "Can't tell by the handwriting—'cause there isn't any."

"Either way. They're pretty mad...."

"I know, but I mean, come on, it's just a book!" A____ shook her head. "So they didn't like the ending, so what? I can't believe they got so upset about it."

"I can...." muttered Z____, thinking about his own equally enraging experience reading the end of the Series of Secrets. "Hey, what if this guy came in here and saw the same thing we saw?"

"What? All the _____ wrappers?"

"No, the empty notebook."

"And then they got even madder because there was no sixth book?"

Z____ nodded.

"Right. And then..." A____ trailed off.

They stared at each other, both contemplating the horrible possibilities.

Could the X-fan have kidnapped I.B.? Or worse?

OK, author, it seems A____ and Z____ now have their first suspect: the X-fan. What do they do next?

I expect any detectives worth their salt would inspect the suspect's letter for clues about its writer. Where might this prospective villain be? What exactly is he or she trying to say? Who *is* the X-fan? Perhaps A____ and Z____ try to determine which magazines or newspapers were cut up to make the letter?

WRITE THIS:

Take a stab at writing this moment of epistolary sleuthing. You can start however you like, but you should end this section by having your heroes discover a hidden message in the letter. Don't worry, there *is* a hidden message for them to find. (I should know—I left it there.) Of course, you must find it first in order to write about it. Hint: what they fear most is that a *capital* crime has occurred.

Here's the letter again for your reference:

2 ib u stink, 5 bOoks waiTing
for tHe secret and that's all
i gEt? What the heck was
that? u betteR write another
book or elSe I'll senD
u 2 U know wherE.
i'm watching u!
frum yr   X-

The Case of the Missing Author
Chapter 4 (cont.)

In which the young detectives discover a hidden message in the X-fan's letter.

How did that go? Did you—or rather did your heroes—discover the hidden message? Together, the capital letters in the X-fan's letter spell *OTHER SIDE*, correct?

You better write another book or else I'll send you to you know where.

Does *you know where* mean the Other Side? Very likely. After discovering the hidden message, A____ and Z____ must fear that the author of the letter—the X-fan—has sent I.B. to the Other Side.

But what is the Other Side?

Often, the phrase *the other side* refers to the afterlife, the side of the dead. And your heroes will have to consider the grisly possibility that I.B. has been killed. But does the phrase remind you of anything else?

I'm guessing that it will remind A____ and Z____ of something very specific. As readers of I.B.'s books, they will almost certainly remember that the Other Side is where the old magician Italo disappeared to at the end of I.B.'s last book.

The Case of the Missing Author
Chapter 4 (cont.)

"OK, let's say I.B. has been kidnapped and is being held on the Other Side," said A_____. "The question is, other side of what?"

"I think you mean *what Other Side*," said Z_____. "It's not necessarily the other side *of* anything. On the other hand, maybe it's the other side of everything."

"What are you talking about?"

"Remember the end of I.B.'s last book? The Other Side is where Italo disappeared to."

A_____ stared. "So are you saying that the Other Side is real? It's a place? I find that very hard to believe."

"I do, too, but I know this much—if the Other Side *is* real, it's where we're going to find I.B."

A_____ nodded slowly. The Other Side was the only clue they had. They might as well try to find it.

This, then, is your heroes' mission: to find the Other Side and rescue the missing author.

Your mission? The very same.

DEPARTMENT OF PITFALLS:
THE MURKY MIDDLE

No matter how prepared I think I am, I always get stuck near the middle of a book. Usually, it's because I have no idea where my book is going. Even if I know how the book is supposed to end, I don't know how to get there. I spend weeks and weeks, sometimes months and months, flailing around, trying to see my way out of the murky middle. You'd think that after writing five books, I might have developed a technique for avoiding this terrible fate. And, guess what, I have. I'm throwing you into the murk instead. Ready?

No, of course you aren't. See next page.

PROCRASTINATION PAGE

TAKE THREE MONTHS OFF.

TELL EVERYONE YOU NEED TO "RECHARGE."

CREATIVITY REQUIRES REST.

CHAPTER NINE

Genre as Pizza

Next up: how will your heroes find the Other Side?

I'll admit, the Other Side appears to be a somewhat open-ended idea.* Almost as open-ended as fiction itself. There are countless other sides. The other side of the road, of course, but also the other side of the tracks. The other side of the wall. The other side of the coin. The other side of the moon. The other side of a record album. (Also called the B-side; ask your grandparents.) The other side in an argument about the meaning of the other side. The other side of a story.

Each of these other sides could be the basis of a story of its own.

---

*I REFER HERE TO THE OTHER SIDE AS INTRODUCED IN THE ENTIRELY FICTIONAL BOOKS OF THE ENTIRELY FICTIONAL I.B. ANONYMOUS. ANY OTHER SIDE THAT MIGHT OR MIGHT NOT BE MENTIONED IN MY OWN BOOKS IS ENTIRELY BESIDE THE POINT.

Other other sides:

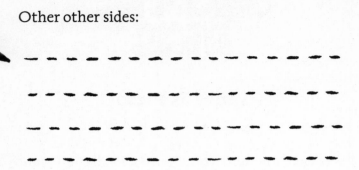

But what is the other side in your book? *The Other Side.* No other other-side matters now. I suppose the Other Side could be the other side *of* your book. As in the back cover. Or even the other side of this page. But I'm guessing you'll want the Other Side to be a place—a place where your heroes can look for the missing author and where they can find... well, that's up to you.

Here's the good news: you get to decide what the Other Side is.

Here's the bad news: you *have to* decide what the Other Side is.

Writing fiction is like that. The best thing about it is that you get to make it up. The worst thing about it is that **YOU HAVE TO**.

So how do you go about deciding what your Other Side is going to be? Or what it is going to be the other side *of*—if indeed it is the other side of something.

Perhaps you have a wholly original concept of the Other Side in your head. If not, here's another side from which to look at the question of the Other Side....

GENRE

In French, *genre* means "kind or sort or type." As in, what kind or sort or type of other side would you like your Other Side to be?

As a literary term, the word has a more particular meaning: a genre is a category of literary works—often but not always novels—defined by form, style, or subject matter. If that sounds vague, well, that's because it *is* vague (and also because the dictionary on my desk isn't very good). Nevertheless, every genre has its own rules and conventions; and while I would never insist that you follow them, I'm sure you'll agree that it's best to know the rules before you break them. Otherwise, you don't get the satisfaction of knowing you've done something wrong.

Also as in, what kind of person would use a pretentious word like that?

117

Think of a literary genre as a type of food. Pizza can be prepared in a myriad of ways, but it's usually round and cheesy and tomato-y and eaten in slices, right? Yes, there are square pizzas and cheeseless pizzas and white pizzas, but those are the exceptions. At a certain point—say, when they start putting barbeque chicken and pineapple on top—a pizza ceases to be a pizza.

(Pineapple pizza is your favorite? Then, please, take my slice.)

Which genre does your book belong to? Well, that's no mystery; as we've already established, it belongs to the *mystery* genre. But let's muddy the genre waters a little bit. (As if the murky middle weren't murky enough!) Yes, this book is a mystery, but it is not only a mystery. Not every book fits comfortably into a single genre; many books combine several genres or don't seem to fit into any at all. I consider my own books to be a unique combination of the true-crime and self-help genres. (They certainly don't help *you*!) Before A_ _ _ _ and Z_ _ _ _ start hunting for additional clues, I want you to choose a secondary genre for your book. The genre you choose will help determine what your Other Side is like and will influence the way you write the rest of your book.

I'm giving you a choice of **three genres:***

1. Classic crime, also known as noir

2. Fantasy

3. Gothic horror

---

*IF YOU LIKE, YOU CAN COMBINE TWO OR THREE OF THESE GENRES, OR EVEN CHOOSE A DIFFERENT GENRE ALTOGETHER, BUT IF YOU DO, YOU'RE ON YOUR OWN. I CAN ONLY KEEP SO MANY POSSIBILITIES IN MIND AT ONCE.

More Genres

In case you're foolish enough to try reading—or writing—another book after this one, here are some other genres you might choose from.

Western (people on horses, gunfights, a lot of cactus)

Science fiction (robots, aliens, dystopian universes where parents are replaced by video screens—wait, is that *dystopian* or *utopian?*)

Romance (the mushy stuff—I'd rather not talk about it)

Sports (I've never read any myself, but I'm told there are actually novels about people chasing balls around a field.)

Graphic novels and manga (at last, a comic book...book!)

Literary (any book your language arts teacher wants you to read)

Coming-of-age (not sure what this means—it never happened to me)

Other genres: _ _ _ _ _ _ _ _ _ _ _ _ _ _

_ _ _ _ _ _ _ _ _ _ _ _ _ _ _ _ _ _ _

Write This Book—
The Multiplayer Version

If more than one person is reading, or I should say writing, this book at once, then each reader/writer should pick a different genre—and write his or her version of the book accordingly. Whoever gets to the end first... gets to the end first!

He looked about as inconspicuous as a tarantula on a slice of angel food.
—RAYMOND CHANDLER

I've been as bad an influence on American literature as anyone I can think of.
—DASHIELL HAMMETT*

Ever murdered your husband? Robbed a bank? Sold shares in an imaginary company to an innocent old lady?

No? Well, chances are you know a little bit about crime even if you're not a criminal. Let me put that another way. Chances are you know a little bit about crime novels even if you've never read one. Classic crime novels like those by Raymond Chandler and Dashiell Hammett have influenced

---

*RAYMOND CHANDLER WAS AN AMERICAN NOVELIST AND SCREENWRITER FAMOUS FOR HIS NOIR STORIES AND BOOKS. HE MIGHT NEVER HAVE WRITTEN A DETECTIVE STORY HAD THE GREAT DEPRESSION NOT CAUSED HIM TO LOSE HIS JOB AS AN OIL COMPANY EXECUTIVE. OIL COMPANY EXECUTIVE? NO WONDER HE WAS SO GOOD AT WRITING STORIES ABOUT CRIMINALS.... DASHIELL HAMMETT WAS ANOTHER AMERICAN AUTHOR OF DETECTIVE NOVELS AND SHORT STORIES. HE LEFT SCHOOL AT THIRTEEN BUT GOT ALL THE MATERIAL HE NEEDED FOR HIS WRITING WHILE WORKING AS AN OPERATIVE FOR THE PINKERTON NATIONAL DETECTIVE AGENCY. IF THERE IS A MESSAGE IN THAT, I'M NOT GOING TO SPELL IT OUT FOR YOU—BECAUSE I CAN'T.

not only many novels that have come since but also many films and television shows—and no doubt more than a few criminals as well.

These "hard-boiled" mysteries are most often written in *first person* through the eyes of a private eye—that is, from the perspective of a detective. The detective is usually an *antihero*—a cynical tough guy, at least in appearance, who pretends not to care about the people around him. He speaks gruffly, with humorous understatement. A hunter of murderers, the noir detective may not be a killer himself, but he delivers deadly one-liners.

You need not write your book in first person to adopt this kind of voice, however—

What do I mean? Can I show you?

Heh. I know what you're up to—you're trying to get me to write this book for you again. You can't fool me.

No? It's just that you're sure I'll do such a good job?

What can I say? I know I'm being played, but flattery will get you everywhere. Let's go back to *The Case of the Missing Author* and give it a bit of a noir spin.

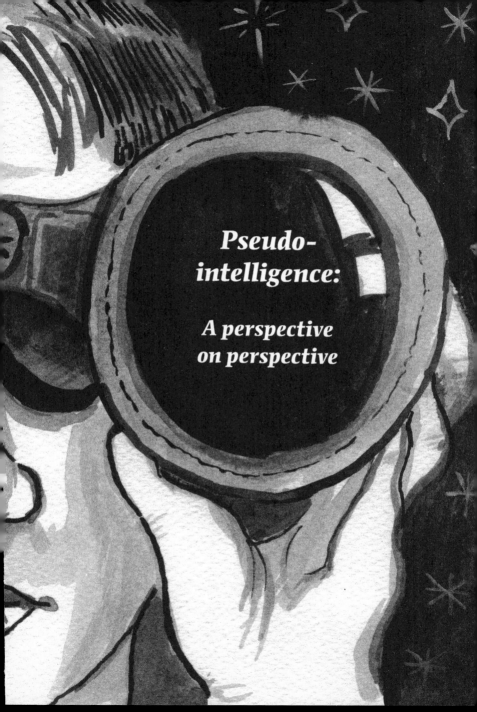

Pseudo-
intelligence:

A perspective
on perspective

No doubt you've heard the word *perspective* before. Parents often tell their children that they should have more perspective. What the parent means is that whatever tragic event has occurred in your life—a bad haircut, say—really isn't so tragic. Your hair will grow back—and besides, children are starving in Africa. It goes without saying that this so-called long view is infuriating for someone whose hair is cut too short. Sure, your hair might grow back *one* day, but will it grow back before school starts next week?

What does this have to do with writing? Everything, my dear innocent young person, everything. In real life, you may not want to enter your parent's head any more than your parent wants to enter yours. As a writer, on the other hand, you are continually called upon to see events from other people's perspectives—that is to say, from the perspectives of all your characters. And if you are writing from your own perspective, it behooves you all the more to consider somebody else's perspective. That way you can anticipate your critics and arm yourself against them.

For writers, perspective—also known as *point of view*—has an additional, more precise meaning. Your perspective is the "person" in which you are writing. As you may already know from your language arts class, in *third person*, the subject is *he*, *she*, or *it*, and the narrator takes little or no part in the action. In *second person*, the subject is *you*—as in the reader. In *first person*, the subject is *I*, and the hero and narrator are generally one and the same. (If you play video games, think of a first-person shooter; the experience is similar, at least if you imagine reading as a gunfight.) A sentence can appear wildly different when written in one person versus another. Take the sentence *He broke the piggy bank*. In third person, it is merely an observation. In second person, it is an accusation: *You broke the piggy bank*. In first person, a confession: *I broke the piggy bank*. How do you know which person to write in? It depends on which person you ask, of course. For the purposes of this book, I (first person) think you (second person) should continue to write about A____, Z____, and I.B. as A____, Z____, and I.B. (i.e., in third person).

And stop whining about that haircut!

Pseudo-assignment: Musical chairs

A game for the whole family! The next time your family sits down for dinner (I know with some families that's a rare event), ask everybody at the table to get up and move to the chair to his or her right. Continue your dinner conversation with each person now playing the part of the original occupant of his or her chair. If you and your family have trouble seeing things from one another's points of view, at least you can have fun with your impersonations. And the writing part? That comes afterward when you write furiously in your journal about the insulting ways your family imitated you.

Now that A____ and Z____ have determined that they need to find the Other Side, I think we can assume that they would take one last look around I.B.'s house—this time for clues about what and where the Other Side might be. Here they are, continuing the investigation like protagonists in a noir mystery:

The Case of the Missing Author
Chapter 5

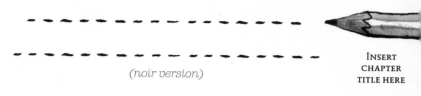

(noir version)

Another day, another crime scene.

Sure, A_ _ _ _ and Z_ _ _ _ were only kids, but they'd cracked enough of I.B.'s old bookamajigs to know how to handle a simple missing-person case like this one. (You want hard, try multiplying fractions—that's hard.) Like old pros, they scoured his office for clues, dusting for fingerprints, checking for hidden doors, all the usual.

Soon enough, they saw it: a body lying behind I.B.'s desk. Glazed eyes. Faded color. If you've seen one dead body, you've seen them all, right?

It was an old stuffed bunny. You know the type. Cute. Cuddly. Covered with ink stains. Some poor kid must have loved this thing once. Now one of his long bunny ears was about to fall off. It would have brought tears to your eyes. That is, if you were the sort who had eyes instead of tiny plastic marbles inset in your fur.

A____ leaned down and picked up the bunny from underneath the desk. His bad ear dangled by a thread.

Z____ looked at her askance. "This is no time for playing with stuffed animals. You're tampering with evidence."

"No, I'm putting him back where he belongs."

Somberly, A____ laid the bunny inside I.B.'s top hat. He looked ready for his funeral. All that was missing was a bunny priest.

A____'s hand lingered inside the hat. "Either I.B. has a really big head or there's a secret compartment in here—"

Z____ stepped closer. "Anything in it?"

His sister pulled out a shiny gold coin with a flourish, playing magician. "Voilà."

Z____ whistled. "That's a lotta gold to hide under a little rabbit. What's it say? Name of a casino or something?"

She handed him the coin so he could read it. They both swallowed as he turned it over.

THE OTHER SIDE, it said on both sides. Like it was some kind of joke. Only it was about as funny as a pimple on picture day.

Beneath the words *THE OTHER SIDE* was something that looked suspiciously like a street address.

The Other Side wasn't on the other side of the moon. It wasn't even on the other side of town. It was right around the corner—

Don't like hard-boiled eggs, let alone hard-boiled crime stories? Don't own a trench coat or even a pair of sunglasses? Perhaps I can interest you in a fantasy, instead....

I doubt that the imagination can be suppressed. If you truly eradicated it in a child, he would grow up to be an eggplant.
—URSULA K. LE GUIN

Do not meddle in the affairs of wizards, for they are subtle and quick to anger.
—J.R.R. TOLKIEN*

You may or may not have meddled in the affairs of wizards, but you almost certainly have meddled with fantasy. If you haven't ever read a fantasy book per se, you must have had a fantasy of your own at one time or another. And if you haven't had a fantasy of your own, well, as the High Queen of Fantasy, Ursula Le Guin, suggests, you must be an eggplant.

---

*THE AUTHOR OF THE EARTHSEA BOOKS, AMONG OTHER FANTASY CLASSICS, URSULA K. LE GUIN SUBMITTED HER FIRST STORY TO A SCIENCE-FICTION MAGAZINE AT THE AGE OF ELEVEN. IT WAS REJECTED. SHE WENT ON TO WIN EVERY SCIENCE-FICTION PRIZE KNOWN TO HUMAN OR ALIEN.... J.R.R. TOLKIEN WAS AN ENGLISH AUTHOR MOST FAMOUS FOR WRITING *THE HOBBIT* AND *THE LORD OF THE RINGS*. THE SURNAME TOLKIEN IS THOUGHT TO COME FROM THE GERMAN WORD *TOLLKÜHN*, WHICH MEANS "FOOLHARDY." HOWEVER, TOLKIEN WAS RECENTLY NAMED ONE OF THE TOP FIVE HIGHEST-EARNING DEAD CELEBRITIES. HE HARDLY SOUNDS LIKE A FOOL.

A fantasy book can be about anything. That's the definition of fantasy, after all. But strangely enough, most fantasy books seem to be about the same things: wizards, witches, elves, dwarves, dragons, and the occasional talking animal. Why? I suppose the curmudgeonly answer would be that most imaginative literature lacks imagination. The more charitable answer, and I think the right one, is that these creatures hold enduring fascination and near-universal appeal. (I say *near*-universal because we all know at least one person who hates fantasy books with a passion.)

Wait—a one-eyed oracle just told me you want to know what a fantasy version of our scene in I.B.'s office would look like. Here's one possibility. I'm sure you can come up with many more.

The Case of the Missing Author
Chapter 5

(fantasy version)

A sudden hush had fallen over I.B.'s office. There was a faint rustling, as if a gentle breeze were passing through the room.

"Did you hear something?" asked A____.

"Why are you whispering?" asked her brother.

A____ felt her pant leg ripple. An old threadbare stuffed rabbit was lying next to her foot. "Hey, it's I.B.'s rabbit."

She picked him up, smiling. "You have to admit, he doesn't look like he can type."

"Ha-ha," said Z____.

"He's kinda cute, though...."

"I am not cute."

"Trust me, I wasn't talking about you," A____ scoffed.

Z____ looked at his sister in confusion. "I didn't say you were."

"You didn't?" She shrugged it off. "Anyway,

aren't rabbits' feet supposed to be lucky? Maybe if we carry him around, we'll find out where the Other Side is."

"Just don't start rubbing my foot. I hate that."

A_ _ _ _ made a face. "That's disgusting."

"That wasn't me!" Z_ _ _ _ protested.

"But there's nobody else here!" A_ _ _ _ glanced down at the rabbit in her hand. Was it her imagination or did the rabbit's tiny plastic eye just blink?

"Would you put me down already?"

A_ _ _ _ jumped—and almost dropped the rabbit.

"Did you...talk?" she stammered. If her brother hadn't also been staring at the rabbit, she would have assumed she was going mad.

"So she's not deaf after all—just rude!" said the rabbit sarcastically. "Now put me down. Please."

"Uh...OK," said A_ _ _ _. In a daze, she started lowering the rabbit to the floor.

"No! Not on that dirty rug." The rabbit shook his head; his floppy ears flailed violently. "Would you want to lie there with all those empty _ _ _ _ _ wrappers?"

"Where, then?" asked A____, trying her best to keep her composure. She hadn't spoken to a stuffed animal in many years, and she'd *never* heard one speak back.

"Where do you think?"

"I think he means I.B.'s hat," said Z____.

"NO, I mean *my* hat!" the rabbit snapped. "Why does everybody always think it's his?"

"Sorry!"

A____ started to put the rabbit in the old top hat.

"Wait! Look inside," said the rabbit.

"But it's empty," said A____.

"Hidden compartment. Don't you know *anything*?" the rabbit scolded. "Never enter a magician's hat without thoroughly inspecting it first."

"I thought it was *your* hat," said Z____.

The rabbit twitched his nose. "Touché."

A____ felt around inside the hat until she found a small object under the lining.

She pulled out a gold key. It gleamed so brightly it seemed to radiate its own light.

"What's this?"

"A magical golden key," the rabbit answered. "Duh."

"We can see that," said Z____. "What's it for?"

"When she puts me in the hat, I'll tell you."

A____ lowered him into the hat, feetfirst. "Well...?" she prompted.

"Didn't you say you were looking for the Other Side?" replied the rabbit, yawning.

"You mean there's a door?" Z____ asked excitedly. "This key will get us to the Other Side?"

"Every door has an other side, doesn't it? That's pretty much the definition of a door."

"You know what he means," said A____. "Is this the key to *the* Other Side? Where they're keeping I.B.?"

"Oh, I think I've given you enough help as it is." And with that, the rabbit closed his plastic eyes. The silk lining of the top hat billowed slightly as he started to snore.

Still staring at the rabbit, A____ and Z____ didn't notice that the walls of the room were vanishing until the shimmering outline of a door appeared in front of them.

What, you don't believe in elves or fairies? What about trolls or dragons? No? Huh. I guess fantasy is not for you. How about a ghost, then? Don't tell me you've never seen a ghost! Well, you're about to....

There are such beings as vampires, some of us have evidence that they exist.
—BRAM STOKER

What terrified me will terrify others; and I need only describe the spectre which had haunted my midnight pillow.
—MARY SHELLEY*

INSERT CHAPTER TITLE HERE

The Case of the Missing Author
Chapter 5

- - - - - - - - - - - - - - -

- - - - - - - - - - - - - - -

(gothic version)

It was a dark and stormy night. Outside I.B.'s house, the wind whistled through the trees—

Stormy night? Oops. It was morning when A____ and Z____ entered the author's house. How much

---

*BRAM STOKER WAS THE AUTHOR OF THE ORIGINAL *DRACULA*, WHICH MEANS HE WAS SOMETHING OF A VAMPIRE HIMSELF (BECAUSE WE ALL KNOW IT TAKES A VAMPIRE TO MAKE A VAMPIRE).... MARY SHELLEY WAS THE AUTHOR OF THE ORIGINAL *FRANKENSTEIN; OR, THE MODERN PROMETHEUS*, WHICH MAKES HER SOMETHING LIKE THE BRIDE OF FRANKENSTEIN, ONLY WITH LESS MAKEUP.

time could have gone by? Normally, your copy editor will catch a mistake like that, but you can't rely on it (especially if you don't have a copy editor). Let's begin another way.

You already know the gothic genre, even if you don't think you do. The tone is eerie. The style is antique. Think *Dracula...Frankenstein...The Headless Horseman*...haunted castles...foggy moors...ghosts...monsters...things that go bump in the night.

Pseudo-intelligence:
Don't use that tone with me

Tone is another term that is difficult to define. But if you think about a tone in music, or even a ring tone, then you can imagine what tone might mean in a literary context. A writer's tone might be light and tinkly or heavy and tragic. Gentle and kind or shrill and sarcastic. Naive and childlike or self-serious and pedantic. Establishing a tone can be a matter of grammar and word choice (or *diction*, to use the literary term). Or it can be a matter of subject and style (uh-oh, another vague word). In the end, tone is subjective. Meaning that while one reader may hear a tone, another may be tone-deaf.

Often, a gothic story will include reference to a spooky legend of some kind, usually a legend dismissed as silly by characters in the story until they are forced to reckon with its veracity. "History and mystery," some call it:

The Case of the Missing Author
Chapter 5

INSERT
CHAPTER
TITLE HERE

(gothic version)

"Look at this!" shouted Z____, trying to make himself heard over the howling winds.

He pointed to the legs of I.B.'s desk. They were gouged all over, as if somebody had taken a screwdriver to them. "You think the cat did that?"

"I don't know, it looks more like tooth marks than scratches," said his sister, frowning.

Z____ smiled darkly. "The Were-Hare, then."

"Right. That's what got I.B. Not a crazed fan— a rabid rabbit." A____ laughed, but she felt a chill nonetheless.

Like all the children in the neighborhood, A_ _ _ _ and Z_ _ _ _ had grown up hearing strange stories about the Were-Hare, the monster rabbit who allegedly haunted the woods behind their street. According to legend, the Were-Hare had teeth of gold, so long they reached below his chin. Anybody bitten by the Were-Hare went mad—and believed for the rest of his life he was a rodent in human form. On the other hand, anybody who managed to extract one of the Were-Hare's teeth would have good luck for as long as he could keep the tooth.

Their inspection of the tooth marks was interrupted by a loud hissing sound. They spun around to see I.B.'s cat standing in the doorway, his back arched to its maximum height and his hair bristling in alarm. In the background, haunting organ music began to play.

Not the Were-Hare again! Either you really believe that story or you're deliberately tormenting me!

"What's wrong with him?" asked A_ _ _ _ .

"Uh, maybe it has something do with that?"

Eyes wide, Z_ _ _ _ nodded his head: something was moving under a pile of papers.

As the cat darted away, whatever it was headed toward Z____ like a wave in a paper ocean.

Before A____ could respond, it sprang into the air, sending papers flying in all directions and casting a monstrous shadow on the wall. It landed at Z____'s foot and opened its mouth—

"Aack!" Z____ jumped away just before the creature could bite into his ankle.

It was the Were-Hare.

His red eyes stared furiously. His pink nose twitched menacingly. His gold teeth gleamed ominously.

"Back! Shoo!" cried Z____. "A____, do something!"

"Like what?"

The rabbit flew at Z____ again. Z____ moved his leg just in time.

A____ picked up the nearest object.

"Not that!" yelled Z____. "That's I.B.'s next book!"

"I'm trying to save your life! Besides, it's blank, remember? He didn't write a thing!" said A____, swatting at the rabbit with the notebook.

The rabbit chomped down on the notebook in a rage. A____ tugged hard, but the growling rabbit sank his teeth in deeper.

"You get out of here, you nasty rabbit!"

A____ spun around, lifting the rabbit into the air. Then she let go.

The rabbit sailed across the room. He landed in the corner with a crash and sagged to the floor.

As his snarls turned to snores, the notebook dropped out of his mouth, a single gold tooth lodged in its side.

Tentatively, Z____ tiptoed over and picked up the notebook, then scurried back to the other side of the room as fast as he could.

"What are we going to do with him?" whispered A____.

"I don't know. But if the stories are true, this tooth might just get us to the Other Side."

Grimacing, Z____ pulled the gold tooth out of the notebook. As he held it up, lightning flashed outside, illuminating the tooth with a fierce golden fire.

READR, CAN YOU PLE ASE EN TE
R TA N Y R SE LF FIR A MOMENT? I
HVE TO R UN AFTR MY RABIT. I'LL
STIC IN A FEW FILLR PAGES TO KEEP
U OCCUPID. SORY, FO R THE BA D
TYP ING.. JUST IN A HRRY, THAT'S
ALL. I TYP GREAT. RLY. THT'S JUS A
VICUS RUMR THAT I DON KNO HOW!

*I BELIEVE MY ERSTWHILE AMANUENSIS (THAT MEANS "FORMER WRITER'S
ASSISTANT," IF YOU'RE WONDERING) IS HERE QUOTING FROM SHAKESPEARE'S
MERCHANT OF VENICE. NOBODY EVER ACCUSED THAT RABBIT OF NOT HAVING
A FLAIR FOR THE DRAMATIC.

RANDOM WRITING TIP:
When in doubt,
INSERT FART JOKE.

- -

- *

*MAN, THAT JOKE STINKS! (THANK GOODNESS MOST WRITERS WRITE IN PRIVATE, WHERE NOBODY CAN SMELL THEM.)

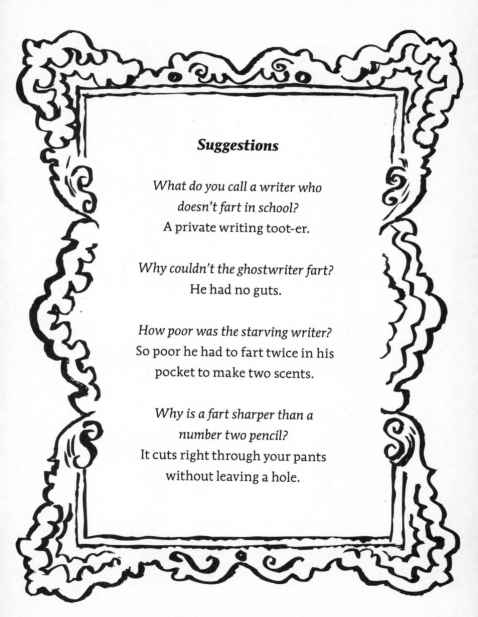

Suggestions

What do you call a writer who
doesn't fart in school?
A private writing toot-er.

Why couldn't the ghostwriter fart?
He had no guts.

How poor was the starving writer?
So poor he had to fart twice in his
pocket to make two scents.

Why is a fart sharper than a
number two pencil?
It cuts right through your pants
without leaving a hole.

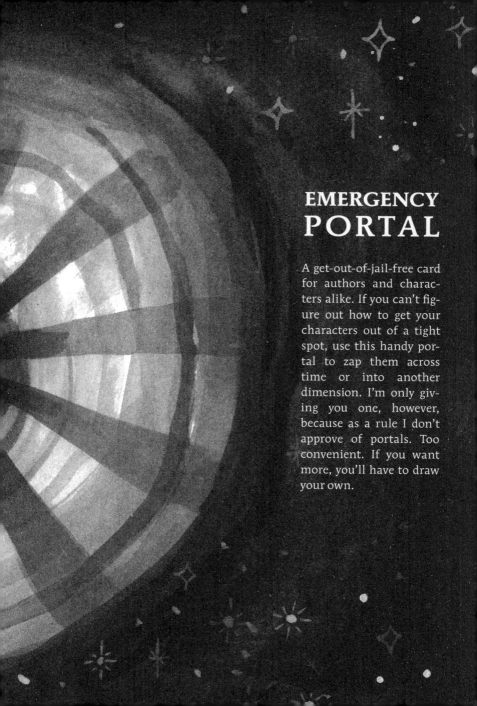

EMERGENCY
PORTAL

A get-out-of-jail-free card for authors and characters alike. If you can't figure out how to get your characters out of a tight spot, use this handy portal to zap them across time or into another dimension. I'm only giving you one, however, because as a rule I don't approve of portals. Too convenient. If you want more, you'll have to draw your own.

Dear Guest,

We regret to inform you of a staff change. After years by our side, our longtime companion Quiche has decided it's time to explore greener pastures, or should we say orange-er carrots. It saddens us to see him go, but we wish him the best of luck in his new endeavors, and we want him to know our hat is always open to him should he choose to return. While we search for a replacement, we will attempt to offer the same excellent service you've come to expect. As we ourselves are now forced to type and retype and, er, retype our words again, you may experience a slight delay in your reading. Please bear with us.

—The Management

CHAPTER TEN

Fictional Worlds: The Other Side

Are you ready? This is it—it's time for you to enter the Other Side. By which I mean, it's time for you truly and finally to take over my side, the writer's side. You're not a beginner anymore, and I'm done holding your hand—it's much too clammy.

Depending on the genre you've chosen—noir, fantasy, or gothic—your heroes now have the coin, key, or tooth that will gain them entrance to the Other Side.

What is the Other Side like? It's up to you. Following are some suggestions—but they are only suggestions.

Pseudo-intelligence:
The whole world in your hands

A novel doesn't just tell a story; it describes a world. By world I mean the location of your story, but also something less tangible. The world of your book might be the kind of place where an elf or tree sprite or leprechaun is likely to pop up. Or it might be the kind of place where you're more likely to see a nurse or insurance salesman or social studies teacher. It might be familiar or exotic. Funny or scary. Urban or rural. All gray or colored in neon. The world of your book might be as small as a box of takeout from a Chinese restaurant, or as large as an ocean. (Of course, to a microbe the takeout box might seem enormous, and to a giant squid the ocean might seem small.) Generally speaking, the only rule about fictional worlds is they should be consistent in and of themselves; Middle-earth is Middle-earth, and middle school is middle school, and never the twain shall meet. Then again, it is when worlds collide that new worlds are created....

Pseudo-assignment: When worlds collide

Think of two very different worlds (like Middle-earth and middle school) and imagine one inside the other. How would they affect each other? What new world would be born? Write a description of this new world. If you're inspired, write a story that takes place within it.

NOIR:
A CRIMINAL UNDERWORLD

In a crime novel, I should think that the Other Side would be part of the criminal world—what is sometimes called the *underworld.** But which underworld? An underworld of mafia capos who play poker in pizza joints? An underworld of ragamuffin orphan pickpockets? An underworld of highly paid assassins? To me, the idea of a gold coin, not to mention I.B.'s top hat and bunny, evokes the presence of a magician, or magicians.

---

*THIS CRIMINAL UNDERWORLD IS NOT A LITERAL, UNDERGROUND UNDER-WORLD, SUCH AS YOU MIGHT FIND IN GREEK MYTHOLOGY OR UNDERNEATH A GOPHER HOLE. ALTHOUGH IT'S TRUE THAT PLENTY OF GREEK GODS—AND PLENTY OF GOPHERS—ARE KNOWN TO HAVE BEEN CRIMINALS.

What if your underworld belongs to criminal street magicians who amaze you with coin tricks—and rob you at the same time? You know, those masters of three-card monte who haunt the street corners and back alleys of big cities around the world.* What else might you find in a place like this? People selling stolen goods, maybe, as well as other street performers, like jugglers or mimes. Rats of the human and animal variety. Assorted trash. Grime.

As for the business advertised on the gold coin—the Other Side itself—it would be the magicians' club or pool hall or other seedy establishment of your choosing where the criminal magicians congregate between cons. As you will remember, it's right around the corner from I.B.'s house. To get there, A____ and Z____ have only to walk. Getting inside? Well, that's another matter. I suppose the coin may get them in—but as honored guests or suspicious outsiders?

---

*THREE-CARD MONTE IS A "SHELL GAME" INVOLVING THREE CARDS. THE PERFORMER—TYPICALLY, A STREET MAGICIAN—SHOWS YOU A CARD, THEN ASKS YOU TO FOLLOW THE CARD AS HE MOVES IT AND TWO OTHER CARDS AROUND ON A TABLE. AT THE END, YOU CAN'T PICK OUT THE ORIGINAL CARD, AND YOU BLAME THE SPEED OF THE PERFORMER'S HANDS. IN FACT, THE SPEED DOESN'T MATTER AT ALL; HE HAS SWAPPED THE ORIGINAL CARD WITH ONE OF THE OTHER TWO CARDS AT THE VERY BEGINNING. NEVER LET YOURSELF GET LURED INTO A GAME OF THREE-CARD MONTE. YOU WILL LOSE. UNLESS, OF COURSE, I'M THE ONE DEALING THE CARDS. ME YOU CAN TRUST. NOW PUT YOUR DOLLAR ON THE TABLE AND WATCH CLOSELY....

NOIR FLAP COPY*

Circle the words that best fit the noir world of your imagination, then use them to describe in riveting detail the gritty noir novel you are writing.

Adjectives:	Nouns:	Verbs:
gritty	alley	cheat
dark	shadow	slug
sly	trench	steal
sluggish	con man	lie
cruel	eyebrows	shatter
soft-spoken	fedora	slip

- - - - - - - - - - - - - - - - - - -

- - - - - - - - - - - - - - - - - - -

*FLAP COPY IS THE WRITING, OR "COPY," THAT GOES ON THE FLAP OF A BOOK COVER. IT'S SUPPOSED TO ENTICE YOU TO READ (OR, MORE TO THE POINT, BUY) THE BOOK DESCRIBED. TRUTH AND ACCURACY NOT ESSENTIAL.

FANTASY:
A MAGICAL UNDERWORLD

Dorothy waking up to discover Oz outside her door...the Pevensie kids stepping out of the wardrobe into the snowy night of Narnia...Harry stepping onto the Hogwarts Express...The moment when a character crosses from the everyday world into a world of fantasy is always thrilling—at least for a reader who likes fantasy.

When we left A_____ and Z_____, a shimmering door had just materialized in the middle of I.B.'s office. What lies on the other side of this door?

Perhaps the fantasy Other Side is a parallel universe that is the mirror image of ours. Or perhaps it's nothing like ours; it's a place where the earth revolves around the moon, gravity pulls you up into the sky, and people hang upside down like bats. The possibilities are many—maybe too many.

Let's narrow them down by taking our cue from the stuffed rabbit—the only emissary of this Other Side we've met. What if, like Alice's White Rabbit, the stuffed rabbit heralds from an underland wonderland? When your heroes unlock the shimmering door with the gold key, they find a staircase that goes down, down, down, far below where they can see. (The rabbit skips the stairs; he simply dives through the hole in his top hat.) What do your heroes find when they get to the bottom—aside from a lot of chewed carrots? Other toys or stuffed animals come to life underground? An advanced civilization of giant sentient earthworms? A world of glittering gold mines and crystal caves and magical underground lakes inhabited by dwarves, elves, and mermaids who have never seen the sun?

I say yes, yes, and yes.

FANTASY FLAP COPY

Circle the words that best fit the fantasy world of your imagination, then use them to describe in glowing detail the magical fantasy novel you are writing.

Adjectives:	Nouns:	Verbs:
magical	sword	pummel
epic	sorcery	swashbuckle
luminous	dungeon	roar
heroic	druid	divine

- - - - - - - - - - - - - - - - - -

- - - - - - - - - - - - - - - - - -

GOTHIC:
A DARK FOREST

Close your eyes and you can imagine any number of gothic landscapes: deserted ocean bluffs, rocky caves, blind alleys, medieval villages, crumbling castles. But I'm going to push you in the direction of a dark and mysterious forest. Why? Do you happen to remember the howling at the end of the prologue? Did that spark your imagination when you read about it? Does it make you think of anything now? The Were-Hare, of course. Maybe a were*wolf*, as well? Maybe a pack of werewolves? And, yes, werewolves can go anywhere, but home base is usually a forest, I believe. A forest full of creatures that come out only at night. The gold tooth? Let's call it a talisman for now. A good-luck charm. Perhaps one of your heroes could fasten it to a chain and wear it for protection...against bad writing, if nothing else.

GOTHIC FLAP COPY

Circle the words that best fit the gothic world of your imagination, then use them to describe in electrifying detail the haunting gothic novel you are writing.

Adjectives:	Nouns:	Verbs:
uncanny	blood	raise
cursed	requiem	brood
haunted	tooth	transform
putrid	coffin	lurk
hairy	bat	horrify
seductive	wing	electrify

WRITE THIS:

OK, you've had a chance to think about what your Other Side might be like. Three chances, to be exact. Now it's time to commit to your vision. In the space below, take your heroes from the familiar confines of their neighborhood to the exciting new world of the Other Side. What is the first sight that greets your heroes as they cross the threshold to the Other Side? Do they get only a teasing glimpse? Or do they see a vast panorama? It's your job to point out the sights of this new world in the way you think will be most compelling for your reader—and most fun for you.

The Case of the Missing Author
Chapter 6

INSERT CHAPTER TITLE HERE

- - - - - - - - - - - - - - - -

- - - - - - - - - - - - - - - -

In which A____ and Z____ cross to the Other Side for the first time.

- - - - - - - - - - - - - - - -

PROCRASTINATION PAGE

DOODLE.

STARE AT DOODLE.

THINK, HEY, THIS DOODLE ISN'T SO BAD—
MAYBE I SHOULD BE A CARTOONIST,
NOT A WRITER.

STARE AT DOODLE AGAIN.

MAYBE IT'S NOT SO GREAT AFTER ALL.

GO BACK TO WRITING.

CHAPTER ELEVEN

A Trail of Chocolate:
Keeping Your Book on Track

I have a question for you. No, not *what comes next?* (That comes next.) The question is *what came last?* Where did you leave your heroes?

Yes, yes, I know, you left them on the Other Side, and that's very thrilling, of course, but what else is happening story-wise? Wait, don't tell me, the intrepid brother and sister are fighting over how to start hunting for I.B.—yes, that must be it. No? You mean they've lost sight of each other already? Each of them is alone and bewildered in a new world? Nope? Then has one of your heroes fallen into a hole or been caught in a trap? Oh, I know! They're so intoxicated by their new environment that they've forgotten who they are and what they're supposed to be doing! The old hypnotized-by-the-wonderfulness-of-it-all twist. Very clever of you.

No, none of those things, either? OK, I give up. Your story must be very original if I can't imagine—

Pseudo-assignment:
Understatement and hyperbole

Imagine a shocking event—a horrendous crime, a massive natural disaster—and write about the event as if it were the most ordinary and humdrum thing in the world. Then imagine an ordinary event—a piece of bread toasted, a tooth brushed—and write about it as if it were terribly shocking and momentous.

What? You're not telling me A_ _ _ _ and Z_ _ _ _ are still "soaking it all in"? They're marveling at the sights and sounds of the Other Side? You mean like tourists? Huh. We're going to have to do something about that. Could get boring real soon, my friend. Remember, this isn't serious literature we're writing here; it's genre fiction. We need action. There's nothing more deadly to a story than an aimless hero.

Even when your heroes are distracted from their mission (whether voluntarily or by force), you want to keep the mission somewhere in their minds and in the minds of your readers. Remember our plot map? Your heroes are on the road now. Destination: story climax. It's not that I am against exploring side streets and off-road attractions—on the contrary, I often feel that writers are most on target when they are off topic*—but your little side trips are much more likely to hold your reader's interest if your reader has some sense of where your story is going. Ultimately, whatever your Other Side looks like, A____ and Z____ will have to continue their investigation there, whether that means looking for clues or simply asking people if they've seen I.B.

*An off-topic footnote: OFF TOPIC means "off the subject," but not necessarily OFF THE WALL (which I'm sure I don't have to define for you) or OFF-COLOR (which I probably shouldn't define for you). My aside about the expression OFF-COLOR was OFFHANDED, meaning it was a casual remark, rather than something with a lot of thought put into it. (In that sense, this whole book is offhanded.) OFFAL refers to parts of an animal not usually eaten, like the intestines (sometimes called innards or tripe) or the pancreas (sometimes called sweetbreads). Some people consider offal a delicacy; others might think it tastes something awful. (Nothing, however, could leave as bad a taste as that terrible pun.) If food is OFF, it's spoiled. If a person is OFF, he's a bit suspicious-seeming. Or else he's just not as ON as he usually is. Somebody who's always on is somebody who's always performing, always trying to get a laugh—even when he's not very funny. (I'm not naming names.) If something is JUST PLAIN OFF, it's all wrong, or at least a little bit IFFY. (I have never heard of anything being OFFY, but if you'd like to use the word, give it a try.) An OFFICE, as you know, is not just a place of work, it's also a position held, such as the office of the President or the office of the Class Clown. If someone is OFFICIOUS, he is too by-the-books and rule-oriented, and we don't like him. If he's OAFISH, then he's probably a dolt. A person who falls OFF THE WAGON is a drunk who was trying to stay sober but can't help having a drink. If somebody goes OFF ON YOU,

WRITE THIS:

Continue where you left off—or better yet, ruthlessly cut the last section and start over at the point your heroes enter the Other Side. They are alone in an unfamiliar world. And yet against all odds they must try to catch the scent of I.B. The author's appearance on the other side must have left some kind of impression, right?

Hmm, what could I.B. have left that your heroes might notice? What special characteristic or habit does he have that might leave a trace? You guessed it. Chocolate. I suggest your heroes follow a trail of chocolate. Or a trail of chocolate wrappers, anyway. (The chocolate itself I'm sure I.B. would have eaten.) Think of Hansel and Gretel. I.B. has strewn _____ brand chocolate bar wrappers in his wake—intentionally or unintentionally—the way Hansel and Gretel leave a trail of crumbs on their way into the Black Forest.

Where does the trail lead? Only time will tell.

HE'S PROBABLY ANGRY AND SAYING MEAN THINGS TO YOU. HE MAY EVEN BE *TELLING YOU OFF*. IF HE'S *OFF TO WORK*, HE'S GOING TO WORK. BUT IF HE'S *OFF WORK*, HE'S ON VACATION. HE MIGHT EVEN BE TRYING TO *WORK OFF* SOME POUNDS. BY NOW YOU MUST THINK I'M A LITTLE *OFF CENTER* OR *OFF BALANCE*, IF NOT DOWNRIGHT *OFF MY ROCKER*—UNLESS I'M COMPLETELY *OFF TARGET* AND YOU'RE FOLLOWING MY THINKING, IN WHICH CASE YOU MUST BE AS OFFY AS I AM. BUT SOMETIMES IT IS BY *TURNING OFF* YOUR CRITICAL FACULTIES, BY ALLOWING YOURSELF TO VEER *OFF COURSE*, BY NOT *CUTTING OFF* A MEANDERING CHAIN OF THOUGHT (OR DO YOU PREFER *TRAIN* OF THOUGHT? *TRAIL* OF THOUGHT? *STREAM* OF THOUGHT?) THAT THE MOST CREATIVE IDEAS EMERGE. SOMETIMES. OK, THAT'S IT, I'M DONE *SOUNDING OFF*.

The Case of the Missing Author
Chapter 6 (cont.)

In which A____ and Z____ follow a trail of _____ brand chocolate bar wrappers.

Fantastic. I can tell you're becoming a better writer by the minute!* Nonetheless, I'm going to close this chapter for you. Just to maintain momentum. (And because there's a little plot point I want to insert.) As always, feel free to rewrite my words with your own.

*I KNOW, I PROMISED I WOULD STOP SHOWERING YOU WITH EMPTY PRAISE. SORRY.

The Case of the Missing Author
Chapter 6 (cont.)

By now they had been searching for hours without finding another _____ bar wrapper. Could this be the end of the trail? A_ _ _ _ and Z_ _ _ _ wondered. Would they ever find I.B. in this new world, or were they doomed to wander the Other Side forever?

Suddenly, they heard a noise coming from close behind them.

They spun around to see the silhouette of a stranger blocking their way.

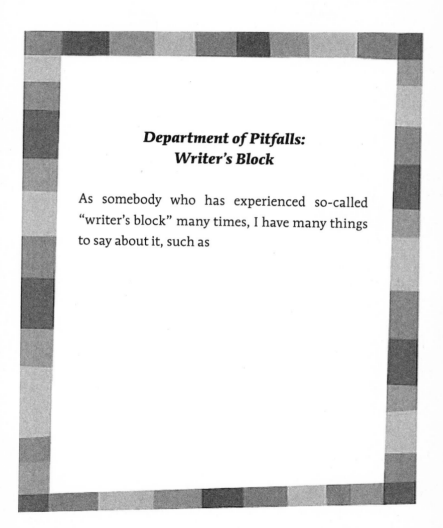

Department of Pitfalls:
Writer's Block

As somebody who has experienced so-called "writer's block" many times, I have many things to say about it, such as

CHAPTER TWELVE

A Side of Fries

There comes a time in every writer's life when he doesn't know what to write. (Actually, there come many such times, but my point stands.) I have heard numerous solutions to this basic problem, including the aforementioned fart joke (see pages 152–153), but my favorite belongs to Raymond Chandler: "When in doubt, have a man come through the door with a gun in his hand."

Unfortunately, this is a kids' book. There can't be any guns in it. Same goes for what is euphemistically called *language*.* If you start writing about characters shooting guns, or even shooting their mouths off, you know what will happen: *I'll* get in trouble. (I know, you've been playing with guns since you were three and you've had a potty mouth for just as long. Sorry. Doesn't matter.) Please save

---

*When I first started writing books for young people, my publishers told me there couldn't be any "language" in my books. How can I write a book without language, I asked, very confused. Is it supposed to be all pictures? It turned out they meant "bad" language. For instance, I wasn't supposed to use the word—oops! I'd better stop before I put my footnote in my mouth.

all that stuff for when you're seventeen years old and you're already causing your parents so much grief they can't be bothered with the likes of me. For now, keep it clean.

Even so, gun or no gun, it's not a bad idea to have a new character walk into your story every now and then. Every book needs a side character or two. A side character is the French fries to your hero's hamburger; he turns your book into a full meal.

What sort of side character should you include in your book? Well, it could be a sidekick, of course. I'm sure you're familiar with the idea of a sidekick.

Pseudo-intelligence:
Foiled again!

A *foil* is a character who differs from another character in a way that highlights the other character's attributes (whether positive or negative). Sherlock Holmes, for example, is tall and so consumed with his cases that he can go for days without food or sleep; his shorter, rounder, and more cautious friend Watson, on the other hand, is the type never to miss a meal. I don't have to tell you which of those two I most resemble. What? No, not Watson! Sure, I like a good meal as much as the next guy, but consider my razor-sharp Sherlockian mind....

Batman's Robin. The Lone Ranger's Tonto. Sherlock Holmes's Watson. A magician's rab—well, never mind that one. A sidekick provides a *foil* for your hero and gives your hero somebody to bounce ideas off of. (A sidekick can do the same for a villain, of course.) For those things, your heroes A____ and Z____ already have each other, however; in a sense, they are each other's sidekicks.

Happily, there are many other kinds of side characters. Among other things, a side character can:

a) threaten your hero with violence or
   some other sort of undesired outcome
b) tempt your hero to do something he
   knows he shouldn't do
c) provide information your hero needs
   to reach his goal
d) serve as a guide in a new world such as
   the Other Side (I guess that would be
   an Other Side character)

For your new side character, I suggest e) all of the above. And let's make him a suspect in our ongoing mystery to boot.

Allow me to introduce him to you:

Remember the stranger who appears at the end of the last chapter? Guess who it is. That's right. Your side character. Literally blocking the way out, he is also one of the first obstacles that your heroes confront on their mission. (For your story's sake, I hope there will be many more.) By following the trail of chocolate, A____ and Z____ have attracted unwanted attention. Instead of leading them to I.B., the trail of chocolate has led someone else to them.

And guess what he has in his hand. No, not a gun. It's a cig—wait, we're not supposed to have those in the book, either! Well, just watch what happens....

INSERT
CHAPTER
TITLE HERE

The Case of the Missing Author
Chapter 7

In which your heroes meet your side character.

The stranger stared at them, puffing on a cigarette, not saying anything. He was about fifteen or sixteen. It was hard to tell exactly.

"I'm Rufus," he said, as if they should have known. "What do they call you where you're from?"

A_ _ _ _ and Z_ _ _ _ squeaked out their names.

Z_ _ _ _ nodded at Rufus's cigarette. "You must have a death wish," said Z_ _ _ _, trying not to show any fear.

Rufus laughed. "Are you talking about this?" He puffed on his cigarette, and a white cloud came out. But it was a cloud of powdered sugar, not smoke.

He held out the cigarette for them to inspect. It had a pink rubbery end. "It's bubble gum, you dummies. I'm using it to quit."

"You're quitting smoking? That's good," said A_ _ _ _.

"No, I would never smoke. I meant quit chewing gum.... Now give me the gold."*

"What gold?" asked Z_ _ _ _ nervously.

"The gold you flashed to get into this place. The

☐ coin."

☐ key."

☐ tooth."

---

*PHEW, NOT A REAL CIGARETTE. ANOTHER BULLET DODGED. OH, WAIT—NO BULLETS!

"Say we have it—why should we give it to you?" asked A_____.

"You're looking for I.B., aren't you? Or were you just collecting _____ brand chocolate bar wrappers for fun?"

Z_____ opened his mouth in surprise. "You know where he is?"

"I might."

A_____ and Z_____ looked at each other. Could they trust him?

All right, author. Take that thinking cap off your pen and put it on your head. It's time for you to flesh out your new character a bit more.

I called him Rufus—maybe because he seems like a rough sort of guy?—but you can call him whatever you like. Is he short or tall? Pale or dark? Does he have an accent? A scar? Green hair? Tattoo?

Clearly, we want Rufus to seem suspicious. He might even be Suspect #1 himself, the X-fan who wrote the threatening letter to I.B. But I think there should be something appealing about Rufus as well. Could he be responsible for

Pseudo-intelligence: Misleading information

A *red herring* is a clue or piece of information that is intended to mislead or distract the reader—for example, an innocent character presented as a suspect. Once, it was believed the expression *red herring* came from the practice of dragging a red herring to lure hunting dogs—but that idea turned out to be a red herring.

I.B.'s disappearance? Maybe. And yet there's also the possibility that he's just a *red herring*. In the end, he could turn out to be a friend and not a foe.

Need more guidance? Let your genre generate your character for you.

NOIR:
A STREET MAGICIAN

If you're writing a crime novel, Rufus should probably be one of those scoundrel street magicians we discussed earlier. When A____ and Z____ hesitate to give him the gold coin, he offers to do a card trick. If they can guess where the ace lands, he'll tell them where I.B. is. If they can't, they give him the coin. Will they take the bait?

FANTASY:
A TEEN DWARF

For the under-land fantasy version of *The Case of the Missing Author*, I suggest a teen dwarf. I can think of plenty of teen vampires and teen were-wolves, even teen elves, but I can't remember any teen dwarves.* Maybe the dwarf Rufus tells A_____ and Z_____ he wants the gold key to escape aboveground and get away from his dwarf parents and the dull routine of cave living. But what is he really after?

---

*THERE SEEMS TO BE SOME DIFFERENCE OF OPINION ABOUT THE PROPER PLURAL FORM OF *DWARF*: IS IT *DWARFS* OR *DWARVES*? SINCE WE ARE HERE TALKING ABOUT IMAGINARY CREATURES, I THINK YOU CAN SAFELY USE EITHER SPELLING WITHOUT FEAR OF A DWARF TAKING OFFENSE.

GOTHIC:
A WERE-TEEN

In the gothic version, there should be something
dark and brooding and dangerous about Rufus. I
like the idea that he is a were-teen but not necessarily a werewolf. Could he be the Were-Hare in
human form? That would explain why he wants
the gold tooth. If you think he really is the Were-
Hare, don't forget to give him some hare-like
(hare-y?) character traits. Then again, he could be
a were-hog or a were-bear. Just not a Care Bear,
please.

WRITE THIS:

Magician, dwarf, or were-person, your side character has one unavoidable duty: to deliver information.

Where is the missing author? Who has I.B. and why? No doubt, A_____ and Z_____ would be full of questions for Rufus.

How do they get him to tell them what they want to know? Here's the most obvious answer: they strike a deal with him. If he tells them where I.B. is, they'll give Rufus the gold object he wants.

The Case of the Missing Author
Chapter 7 (cont.)

In which Rufus is described in detail, then strikes a deal with A and Z—his information for their gold.

OK, did you finish writing the scene with Rufus?

Don't bother pretending—you couldn't have finished it, because you don't know the answers to your heroes' questions. You don't know where I.B. is or even who your villain is. Whether it's the X-fan or somebody else, *someone* must be keeping the infamous anonymous author captive. I'm afraid you'll have to come back and rewrite that last section after you read the next few chapters and gather all the necessary information. Sorry, that's what second drafts are for!

In the meantime, I'll throw in a few paragraphs to keep things moving.

"I still don't understand," said A_____. "Why would anybody take I.B.? He's just a writer. It's just books. You know, like make-believe. Who cares?"

"Make-believe, huh?" Rufus pulled a white glove out of his pocket. "All I know is, I found this in I.B.'s house," he said grimly.

"The Evening Sun—I knew it!" cried Z_____. "They're still trying to learn the Secret."

"But—it can't be one of them—they never take off their gloves," A_____ protested. "How do we know it's not I.B.'s glove—he used to be a magician, right?"

"You think I.B. would wear a white glove, knowing what he knows?" asked Rufus.

"Fine, but how do we know it's not yours?" asked A____, refusing to be convinced.

"Really, you think this is mine?" Rufus put his hand against the glove. The fit wasn't even close.

THE TICKING CLOCK: A RACE AGAINST TIME!

Now A____ and Z____ suspect the worst: that the Evening Sun are responsible for I.B.'s disappearance. The Evening Sun must still be hunting for the Secret—just as in I.B.'s books! This is scarier than the prospect of a deranged fan kidnapping him. Doubtless, something terrible will happen if your heroes don't rescue I.B. soon.

We call this the ticking clock.

POSSIBLE TICKING CLOCKS:

A bomb set to explode in a pickle factory

The world's chocolate supply destroyed

A killer cheese mold loosed upon their home city

Something not to do with food (Now, that would truly be a disaster!)

Or, if you want to go a more predictable route:

NOIR:
The Evening Sun are going
to kill I.B. if he doesn't reveal
the Secret.

FANTASY:
He will be stuck in a fantasy world
forever if he doesn't reveal the Secret.

GOTHIC:
He will be made into a were-hare
if he doesn't reveal the Secret.

WRITE THIS:

Feeling that their mission is more urgent than ever, A____ and Z____ ask Rufus to get them to I.B. as fast as possible. Unfortunately, being young and inexperienced, your heroes have already given Rufus the gold he desires. As a result, he ditches them at the first opportunity. I know, it sounds heartless, but as the author of this book, your responsibility is to put your heroes in the most perilous situation possible. Which means no protective teenager at their side. (Fear not!—we will find a use for Rufus later.)

Alas, this means your heroes will have to find the place I.B. is being held on their own. Worse, you, the author, will have to figure out a way to get them there. What would I do in this awful circumstance? Well, I wouldn't want to think too hard about it, I can tell you that much. I hate having to think about transportation issues when I'm writing. (It always irks me that my underage characters can't drive. How am I ever supposed to get them anywhere?) Never mind the problem of a character not knowing where he's going.

If I were in your shoes, I would probably cheat. After their initial shock at being abandoned by

Rufus, I would have your disgruntled heroes discover that he dropped the villain's glove—along with a scrap of paper on which he has written the villain's address. Too convenient? Then maybe he dropped a map with the villain's location circled? No? Oh, well. Happily for me, the problem is yours, not mine.

The Case of the Missing Author
Chapter 7 (cont.)

In which Rufus takes your heroes' gold and runs away, leaving them to find I.B. on their own.

PROCRASTINATION PAGE

REREAD EVERYTHING
YOU'VE WRITTEN.

DECIDE IT'S ALL TERRIBLE AND
RIP IT UP IN DISGUST.

INSTANTLY REGRET YOUR DECISION
AND PAINSTAKINGLY TAPE YOUR
PAGES BACK TOGETHER.

TELL NO ONE HOW
CRAZY YOU ARE.

CHAPTER THIRTEEN

The Tension Mounts

Where is I.B.?

Rufus has told A____ and Z____ that I.B. is being held captive, but by whom? A dastardly villain, I hope. A nefarious, perfidious, and altogether hideous member of the Evening Sun. I know you're anxious to meet your villain, but before your heroes face their new nemesis, they have to break into his stronghold—where he has stashed I.B. They have to storm the proverbial castle.

So I repeat: Where is I.B.? What is this castle? Where does your as-yet-unseen villain lurk? A lonely laboratory? A forbidding fortress? A lurid lair?

FILL IN THE
DETAILS:
WHAT'S ON
THE SCREEN?

NOIR: AN OLD THEATER

When somebody is tied up in a noir story, it's usually in the trunk of a car, or maybe in a smoky back room, not in a vaudeville theater. But it strikes me that a theater is a likely location for a magician like Rufus to send your heroes. An old theater provides a lot of ammunition for a writer's arsenal: props and sets for your characters to dart in and out of, ropes and curtains for them to be bound with, dressing rooms for them to hide in. To establish a noir feeling, you should make your theater decrepit and run-down. Give the man behind the counter a sinister quality that makes your reader think he's poisoning the popcorn. And if you really want to hit the nail on the head, have an old black-and-white noir movie playing on the screen.

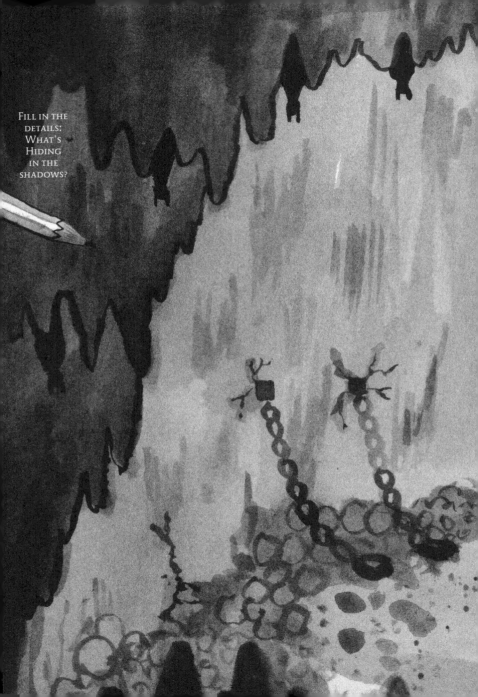

FILL IN THE
DETAILS:
WHAT'S
HIDING
IN THE
SHADOWS?

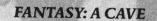

FANTASY: A CAVE

Why fight it? If you're being held prisoner underground, why not be held prisoner in a cave? Shackles and chains are always shown off to great advantage by stone walls. If you feel a plain cave is not fantastical enough, color the walls rosy pink or glowing green. Fill the cave with a silver pool and carve out glittering stalagmites and stalactites. And then for good measure, hide the cave with so many enchantments we fear your heroes will never find it—and that if they find it, they will never get out.

FILL IN THE
DETAILS:
WHAT'S
LURKING IN
THE MOAT?

GOTHIC: AN OLD CASTLE

Here in the gothic story, I think your castle should be a castle. Let it rise out of the mist, a hulking mass surrounded by an impassable moat and impossibly high walls. As your heroes approach, do they risk detection by armored sentinels? Naturally. But in this world human guards are not the scariest adversaries. It is the inhuman creatures behind the castle walls your heroes should fear. Inhuman like were-Rufus...and were-worse.

WRITE THIS (in three parts):

1. THE DARING PLAN

Now that they know where they're going, your heroes plan their daring rescue. This probably involves a stakeout or some other way of ascertaining the layout and daily routine of the theater/cave/castle. A____ and Z____ record what time the doors open, who goes in and out, etc. Once they've analyzed their destination, they need to come up with a way of getting inside. Do they adopt disguises? Forge documents or party invitations? Wear black masks and leotards and descend into the enemy's headquarters with ropes and grapple hooks?

2. THE CASTLE IS STORMED

Hooray! They made it inside. Your heroes should succeed in getting inside the enemy's stronghold—but only long enough to give us a taste of victory. Inevitably, something goes wrong....Do they make too much noise? Are they double-crossed by

Rufus? Perhaps their *fatal flaws* come into play (see character profiles), and A____ or Z____ messes up at the wrong moment, succumbing to temptation or falling victim to his or her own pride....

3. BUSTED!!!

In any event, they are captured. As their arms are pinned behind their backs, they come face-to-face with the villain....

The Case of the Missing Author
Chapter 8

- - - - - - - - - - - - - - - - -
- - - - - - - - - - - - - - - - -

In which A____ and Z____ storm the proverbial castle, only to be caught by enemy forces.

- - - - - - - - - - - - - - - -
- - - - - - - - - - - - - - - -
- - - - - - - - - - - - - - - -
- - - - - - - - - - - - - - - -
- - - - - - - - - - - - - - - -
- - - - - - - - - - - - - - - -
- - - - - - - - - - - - - - - -
- - - - - - - - - - - - - - - -
- - - - - - - - - - - - - - - -
- - - - - - - - - - - - - - - -

Pseudo-assignment:
Outdoor adventure

Many writers have an extreme fear of the great outdoors. This is not surprising given such factors as soft hands, pasty skin, and an attachment to keyboards and unwholesome snack foods. Nonetheless, I advise all writers to make annual excursions into the outside world. Supposedly, a little vitamin D from the sun is necessary to the health and well-being of all non-vampires, but that is not the reason for my advice. Rather, I recommend going outside to gather writing material. I mean that in a very literal sense. Topics to write

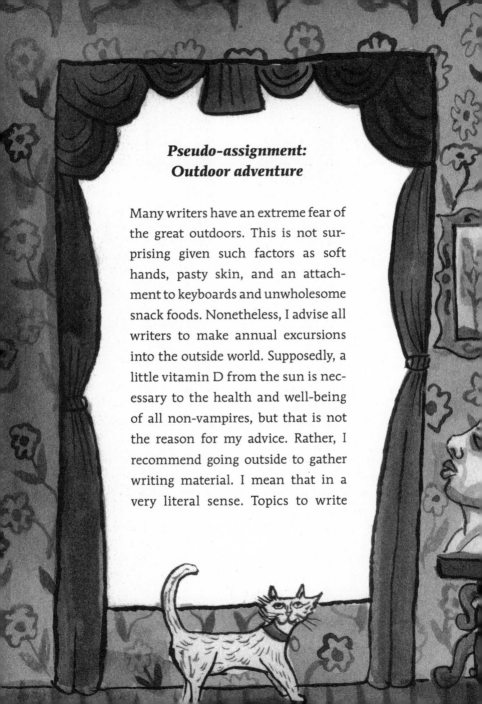

about are readily available indoors. (What is the Internet for, after all?) But what materials are you going to write *with*? After a while you are going to run out of pens, not to mention paper or printer ink. Your assignment: go outside and gather writing materials such as sticks, mud, and leaves. With your new materials, write a secret message to yourself. Or leave a secret message outside for another writer to find. Ideally, the message will be inspired by the materials; and, ideally, the message will be inspiring in turn.

CHAPTER FOURTEEN

Villain: A Good Bad Guy

Every good book has a good bad guy.

Your villain is just as important as your hero; to put it another way, a hero is only as strong as the villain she fights. (Maybe a better word here is *adversary*; but if you don't think of your adversary as a villain, then you're not getting into the proper adversarial spirit.) Your villain keeps the action going. Your villain makes your reader grit his teeth in frustration or clutch her teddy bear in fear. The villain is the source of conflict. And without conflict there is no story. A villain is a writer's best friend.

What makes a good villain? It may seem counterintuitive, but I think it's best to start with your villain's most attractive qualities. What makes your bad guy powerful? Why do other people want to please him? Is it only because they fear him, or does he have some other sort of hold on them?

Of course, your villain might not be a bad guy

in the conventional sense. Your villain might not be a guy at all, or even a gal. Your villain might be monster or mouse, vulture or virus, typhoid or typhoon. You might have an invisible villain or a silent villain. Sometimes the only villain in a book is inside the hero's head. (Have you ever heard someone being described as his or her "own worst enemy"? People say that about me all the time.) But whether your villain is real or imaginary, the same rules apply. Say your villain is the little devil whispering in your hero's ear: ask yourself what makes the devil's voice so much more seductive than the angel whispering on the other side.

Who, then, is your villain?

NOIR:
A MASTER MAGICIAN

Attention, criminals, or, er, crime writers. In classic crime novels, villains usually fall into certain types. Two of the most common are the *Mr. Big* character and the *femme fatale*. Mr. Big is the behind-the-scenes guy who's calling the shots—ordering assassinations and robberies but rarely getting his own hands dirty. Sometimes he'll seem jovial and avuncular at first, maybe offer you a drink or a cigar (that is, if you happen to be a grown-up and living inside an old black-and-white movie). Only at the end do we recognize how ruthless he really is. Likewise, the femme fatale usually enters the story as a victim, not a villain. She plays upon your sympathies and manipulates you into doing her bidding. By the time you realize you've been duped, it's too late.

I don't recommend you model your villain after either of these types, which, after all, are not just types but that awful thing: *stereotypes*. I would go with a more original choice. One of your street magicians, maybe—the sneakiest, smartest, and most talented of the bunch—now off the street and operating his crime ring out of the back of that closed theater. The master magician as master criminal. And if a little Mr. Big slips into his character, you can always tell yourself he's not a stereotype but an *archetype*. It sounds much more dignified.*

As for the missing glove, naturally he pretends that it is only a magician's glove and not a sign that he is part of the Evening Sun. Do you believe him? I don't.

*An *ARCHETYPE* is the original model or ideal form of a type of person, personality, or behavior. A *STEREOTYPE* is the oversimplification or clichéd rendering of a type of person, personality, or behavior. The difference: mostly in the eye of the beholder.

FANTASY:
A HEADSTRONG DRAGON

Fantasists, the characteristics of your alternate universe will most likely determine the character of your villain. If your universe is populated by talking turnips, then your villain may well be a rutabaga. Then again, if your book's alternate universe is more like the one we know in "real

life," then your villain should likewise be more familiar—maybe uncannily familiar. Indeed, if you're writing about a so-called parallel universe, the villain might be the alter ego of the hero, an alternate self.

Of course, if your universe is an utterly fantastical place—as I think your under-land wonderland is—then there is no limit to the form your villain might take. But here again I find that stereotypes often prevail. Why are dragons always so wise? Why are giants always so gentle? Why do so many fantasy characters have names that sound like herbs and not people? (Yes, Eragon, I'm thinking of you.) And why are so many fantasy villains either fiery sorcerers who blacken the world with soot or ice-queen witches who blanket the world with snow?

Your fantasy villain is a cave-dweller, is he not? Then a dragon may be the way to go. Just not a wise dragon, please. Make him rash and headstrong instead. What he's doing wearing a glove with those talons is a mystery to me. Unless the original wearer of the glove is somewhere inside him.

GOTHIC:
AN ALPHA WOLF

Goths, you have an embarrassment of riches when it comes to villains. Not just werewolves but ghosts, witches, vampires (please not the sparkly kind!). They're all yours. Although again, you should watch out for stereotypes. What about a vampire who passes out at the sight of blood? Or a

witch who's terrible at spelling? Or a ghost who's afraid of the dark?

I mentioned werewolves first because, as you know, we've already included a were-animal—the Were-Hare. He could be your villain, I suppose. For all we know, he's coming after A____ and Z____ already, bent on revenging himself and retrieving his lost tooth. But there could also be a nastier creature: an alpha werewolf who rules the castle as an evil lord by day and haunts the woods on four feet at night.

In the case of the werewolf, a dropped glove is easy to explain; it falls off every time his hand turns into a paw.

MWAHAHA:
BUILD YOUR VILLAIN HERE

EVIL MASTER PLAN:
- world domination
- theft of priceless diamond
- to cheat on history final
- to go to Mardi Gras while grounded
- to be voted most popular
- life without parental restrictions
- other _____

TRADEMARK:
- twirling mustache
- eye patch
- evil cackle
- peg leg
- lip balm
- fabulous hair
- other _____

SIDEKICK:
- parrot on shoulder
- lapdog
- drooling, one-eyed ogre
- vacuous beautiful person
- other _____

POWERS:
- turns people to ice or stone with a glance
- necromancer, commands army of zombies
- 12 volts
- killer smile
- morphs into dragon
- excellent hopscotch player
- other _____

BACKSTORY:
- was unloved as a child and therefore hates everyone
- was unloved as a child and therefore insists on being loved by everyone
- was killed many years ago yet refuses to stay dead (and was unloved as a child)
- was hatched out of an egg (and was unloved as a child)
- other _____
  (and was unloved as a child)

Pseudo-intelligence:
How to introduce your villain

Sometimes a villain doesn't appear until late in a story; in earlier parts the villain is only hinted about or indirectly revealed through his actions. In *The Hobbit* and *The Lord of the Rings*, for example, you hear about the terrible doings of the Dark Lord long before you meet him in person (if *person* is the right word for the living embodiment of evil). Other times, you might have a fleeting encounter with a villain at the outset of a novel, perhaps in the guise of a seemingly innocent stranger whose villainy you don't suspect until later—much in the way that someone who meets Bruce Wayne at a party wouldn't suspect he was Batman. In still other cases, somebody your hero sees every day might turn out to be the villain. Even the narrator of a book can turn out to be a villain. Certainly, I've been accused of being a villain more than once. The only rule most people would ascribe to is that your villain must be introduced—or at least mentioned—before the end of your book; it is considered bad form to throw in a villain from outside your book at the last minute simply because you need one.

The Case of the Missing Author
Chapter 9

------ -- -- ------ -- -- -- -- -- -- -- -- -- --

-- -- -- -- -- -- -- -- -- -- -- -- -- -- -- --

In which your heroes meet your villain.

-- -- -- -- -- -- -- -- -- -- -- -- -- -- -- --

-- -- -- -- -- -- -- -- -- -- -- -- -- --

-- -- -- -- -- -- -- -- -- -- -- -- -- -- --

-- -- -- -- -- -- -- -- -- -- -- -- -- --

-- -- -- -- -- -- -- -- -- -- -- -- -- -- --

-- -- -- -- -- -- -- -- -- -- -- -- -- --

-- -- -- -- -- -- -- -- -- -- -- -- -- -- --

-- -- -- -- -- -- -- -- -- -- -- -- -- -- --

-- -- -- -- -- -- -- -- -- -- -- -- -- -- --

-- -- -- -- -- -- -- -- -- -- -- -- -- --

CHAPTER FIFTEEN

The Climax

By now your readers should be gnawing their fingernails and staying up all night with a flashlight, intent on finishing your book. Me, I'm much too old and sleepy to stay awake. If your readers need the rest of the story right away, you'll have to tell the story all by yourself.

Here's what should happen next:

PRISONERS!
Although they intended to rescue a hostage (I.B.), A____ and Z____ have become hostages themselves. They must now face their *greatest fears* (see profiles again). Model yourself on the meanest

substitute teacher you've ever had, and torture your characters as much as possible. If they are claustrophobic, you, the author, must put them in tiny cells where there is no room to stand. If they are afraid of heights, tie them to the top of a tower. If they have a morbid fear of snakes...well, you get the idea.

Mustering all their courage and ingenuity, your heroes must overcome their fears and break out of their prison. How? They can't do it alone. But they can do it with the help of—*drumroll, please*...SUPERBUNNY!

What's that, reader? You think a rabbit super-hero is an unlikely addition to our story? Well, then I guess you've never met MY rabbit!*

Confidential to Quiche:
Faithful furry friend, I admit it, I'm no good without you! You can have as many carrots as you like—and I'll even give you weekends off. Please come back to me!   —Your old pal, P.B.

*IMPORTANT LESSON: SOMETIMES YOU HAVE TO SACRIFICE YOUR ARTISTIC INTEGRITY FOR THE GREATER GOOD.

THE ESCAPE

Once released from their holding cell (thank you, Superbunny!), your heroes use their detective skills and locate the back room/inner cave/dungeon where I.B. is being held captive. With a little bit of luck and more than a little ingenuity (but no bloodshed, please; remember, this is a kids' book!), they avoid being seen and they manage to get inside. There they find a man tied to a chair with his face covered by a hood. I.B.! He doesn't respond to their whispered greeting. Is his mouth gagged? Is he unconscious? Together, A____ and Z____ yank off the hood, revealing . . .

THE TWIST

Rufus! The explanation: Rufus himself was searching for I.B. all along. That was why he wanted the gold coin/key/tooth. Alas, he got caught by the villainous magician/dragon/werewolf, just as A_____ and Z_____ did.

A further twist? <u>Rufus is the X-fan</u>—their first suspect. (How this squares with his identity in the crime world vs. fantasy world vs. gothic world, I leave to you.) He never wanted to hurt I.B., only to push him to write a sixth book. When he discovered I.B. was missing, he, like A_____ and Z_____, embarked on a mission to find him.

What do your heroes do with Rufus? You decide, but I think they would taunt him a little bit (he did ditch them, after all) and demand that he return their gold object before they set him free. Together, they all escape. But not without a few hair-raising moments.

Pseudo-intelligence:
Do the twist

No, not the dance. I'm talking plot twist. You can't have too many twists. Everybody loves a twist.

Famous twists:
XXXXXXXXXXXXXXXXXXXX
XXXXXXXXXXXXXXXXXXXX
XXXXXXXXXXXXXXXXXXXX
XXXXXXXXXXXXXXXXXXXX
Sorry, I didn't want to spoil any of them.

Climax: Defusing the bomb

Now what was your ticking clock? If your heroes' only fear was that I.B. was about to be killed, then it seems your climactic moment has already occurred—and you should beef up the previous section accordingly. (What was the ax that was about to come down on Rufus's neck? How did A____ and Z____ stop it?) If your ticking clock was something else—say, an actual bomb set to explode—now is the time to defuse the bomb. This should be the white-knuckle moment of white-knuckle moments. Let it go down to the wire. All is about to be lost. Your heroes succeed at the very last second. Thankfully, A____ and Z____ now have Rufus to help them. They flee just in time while behind them the villain's theater/cave/castle redoubt is engulfed in flames or collapses on itself or crumbles to the ground....

The end? Not quite.

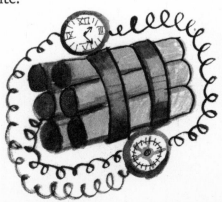

WRITE THIS:

I'm not going to repeat myself anymore. Just write
it below.

The Case of the Missing Author
Chapter 10

INSERT
CHAPTER
TITLE HERE

- - — ~ — — — — — ~ — — — — — — — —

- — — ~ — — — — — ~ — ~ — — ~ — — — ~

*In which A_ _ _ _ and Z_ _ _ _ escape and find the place where
they believe I.B. is being held—only to discover that the prisoner
is Rufus.*

- — — ~ — ~ — — — — — ~ — ~ — — —

— — ~ — — — — ~ — ~ — — — ~ — — ~ —

— ~ — ~ — — ~ — — — ~ — — — ~ — —

— — ~ — ~ — ~ — — — — — ~ — ~ — — ~

~ — ~ ~ — ~ — — — — — — ~ — ~ ~ — —

— — ~ — ~ — ~ — — — — ~ — — ~ — — —

PROCRASTINATION PAGE

(Ending a book is often the hardest part.
I recommend avoiding it as long as possible.)

GO BACK TO FIRST
PROCRASTINATION PAGE.

REPEAT.

THEN WORK YOUR WAY THROUGH
ALL PROCRASTINATION PAGES.

CHAPTER SIXTEEN

Coming Home

A____ and Z____ are now bona fide heroes, and yet they are no closer to achieving their goal. Where is I.B.? Wherever he is, they appear not to have helped him at all.

WRITE THIS:

With or without the help of Rufus, your heroes have to navigate their way home—and then decide what, if anything, to do about finding the missing author. I'll make you a deal: if you get them home, I'll take over the book again from there. Just tap me on the shoulder when you're done, and I'll see if I can manage a few more paragraphs.

The Case of the Missing Author
Chapter 11

*In which A____ and Z____ fight their way out with Rufus,
then find their way home.*

CHAPTER SEVENTEEN

The End—P.B.'s Version

INSERT CHAPTER TITLE HERE

The Case of the Missing Author
Chapter 12

- - - - - - - - - - - - - - - - - - - -

- - - - - - - - - - - - - - - - - - -

(P.B.'s version)

Two days later...

A_____ didn't think about the _____ coming out of I.B.'s chimney until she was already walking back into her house with the day's mail under her arm.

Suddenly, she realized what it meant.

"Z_____!" she shouted, dropping the mail on the floor. "He's back—or somebody is!"

This time they didn't hesitate. They ran across the street and pounded on I.B.'s door.

A muffled voice came from inside. "Hold on—I'm coming!"

Their neighbor opened the door after about a minute and a half. He was wearing pajamas, and his hair was standing on end. His cat protectively circled his feet.

"Oh, it's you guys," said I.B., as if they'd known each other for years. "What's the emergency?"

"We should ask you that," said A_____.

"What do you mean? Everything's fine here."

Z_____ looked at the author suspiciously. "So then…you're OK?"

"Why shouldn't I be? By the way, did you feed the cat like I asked?" He frowned. "He seemed very hungry when I got home."

"The cat? What about you?" protested A_____. "We read your note. We thought you needed our help. We went all the way—"

"We went all the way to the Other Side," said Z_____, finishing his sister's sentence. "We looked all over for you—"

I.B. clapped his hands. "Oh, good. I was hoping you would. What was it like? You have to come in and tell me everything."

"I don't understand—did you want our help or not?" asked Z_____, not moving.

"I absolutely did. I still do," said I.B. indignantly.

"And it sounds as if you have plenty of material for me to write."

"To write?" echoed A____ in surprise.

"Of course. What did you think I needed help with?"

"You wanted us to help write your book?" Z____ spat out. "That's why we let ourselves get messed up with the Evening Sun?"

"Well, yes..."

"You mean you weren't really in trouble?!" asked A____, disbelieving.

"Oh, I was. I am. Big trouble. The book is way overdue and, well, I can't thank you enough—"

A____ and Z____ looked at each other, trying to absorb what the older author was saying.

"But what about what I heard that other night? The laugh and cry and thud?" asked Z____. "You didn't get hurt? They didn't kidnap you?"

I.B. laughed. "Well, I might have hurt my foot when I threw my notebook to the floor.... I was just laughing and crying in despair. Wretched writer's block—it makes me scream every day! Afterward, I went for a walk to clear my head."

"And then you planned it all so we would figure out your story for you."

"Well, I didn't plan it *all*," said the author modestly. "There was a little luck involved."

"So everything we saw and did—saving Rufus—that's all going to go in your book?"

"Oh, that worked, did it?"

"What about everything we saw on the Other Side? Was nothing real?"

"Depends what you mean by that."

"What if we don't tell you our story?"

"Well, I guess you don't have to. But then you wouldn't get the prize," I.B. added nonchalantly.

"What prize?"

"Oh, just membership in the Cester Society…"

Z____'s eyes widened. "Let me get this straight—if we help you write your book, we can be members of the Cester Society?"

"Well, honorary members, anyway."

"It's like our payment?"

"Well, I wouldn't put it so baldly. You make it sound so crass. Like quid pro quo—"

"Wait, we need to talk about it for a second—privately."

I.B. shrugged. The siblings stepped away from his door and heatedly whispered to each other. After a moment, they turned back to I.B. They'd made their decision.

To be continued…

Oh, so you didn't like that ending, either? Well, that must mean this is a good book, then. As a brilliant and distinguished author (OK, it was me) once said, "Only bad books have good endings. If a book is any good, you don't want it to end." To that end, you can keep this book going for as long as you like.

And, who knows, there just might be a membership in a certain secret organization waiting for you…on the other side.

WRITE THIS:

Write your own ending—or endings—here. Attach extra pages as necessary.

The Case of the Missing Author
Ending

(your version)

YOUR LAST ASSIGNMENT

Rewrite everything.

(Because as every writer knows, rewriting is everything!)

THE END*

*Or is it? Don't want it to end?
If you want to keep writing this book, go to
www.thesecretseries.com

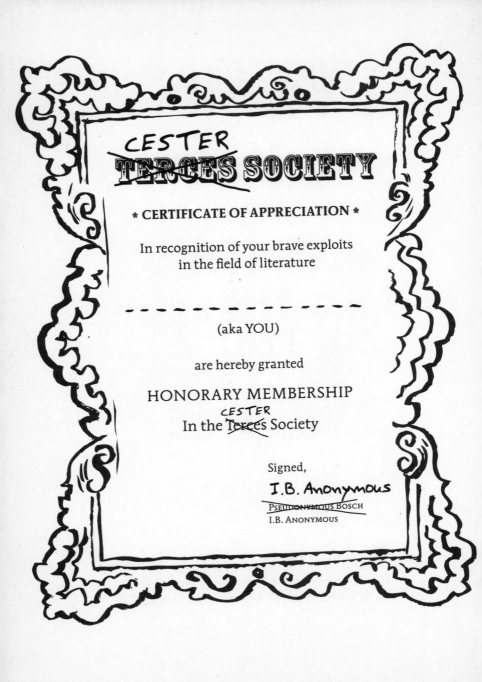

CESTER
~~TERCES~~ SOCIETY

❋ CERTIFICATE OF APPRECIATION ❋

In recognition of your brave exploits
in the field of literature

- - - - - - - - - - - - - - - - - - - -

(aka YOU)

are hereby granted

HONORARY MEMBERSHIP
CESTER
In the ~~Terces~~ Society

Signed,

I.B. Anonymous

~~Pseudonymous Bosch~~
I.B. Anonymous

APPENDIX

Pseudonisms: Words to live by

You don't have to reinvent the wheel every time
you write a book;
you have to reinvent the whole car.

Writers don't get better as they get older;
they just get older.

Don't learn to write. Write to learn.

It's all right to have a lot of books on your plate,
but not on your hot plate—it could start a fire.

Remember, when your face is buried in a book,
nobody can see you pick your nose.

Parental Obituary Section

Anne of Green Gables, by Lucy Maud Montgomery— The eponymous Anne is an orphan adopted inadvertently by a couple who wanted a boy. The cause of her parents' death is unknown.

The Chronicles of Narnia, by C.S. Lewis—Not technically orphans, the Pevensie children are sent to live with their uncle in the country while their parents remain in London for the duration of the war.

Cinderella, folktale—Not an orphan per se, Cinderella is certainly treated like one. Traditionally, her mother died in childbirth and her father only later.

Hansel and Gretel, fairy tale—More literary characters with a dead mother. Their stepmother claims there is not enough money to feed them.

Harry Potter, by J.K. Rowling—Harry's parents died protecting their baby from the evil sorcerer Voldemort. Harry famously bears a scar on his forehead from that fateful day.

Heidi, by Johanna Spyri—Heidi is yet another eponymous orphan heroine, this one in the Swiss Alps.

Huckleberry Finn, by Mark Twain—An American classic about a half orphan. Huck's mother died of unspecified causes. His father is a derelict.

James and the Giant Peach, by Roald Dahl—James's parents were killed by a rhinoceros that had escaped from the London Zoo.

Little Orphan Annie, by Harold Gray—The comic-strip prototype of the musical star. Her parents possibly died in a car accident after giving her up for adoption. Possibly.

The Lord of the Rings, by J.R.R. Tolkien—Hairy-footed Frodo Baggins's parents died in a boating accident when he was twelve. Later, the hobbit hero is adopted by his cousin Bilbo, hero of *The Hobbit*.

The Mysterious Benedict Society, by Trenton Lee Stewart—Reynie Muldoon is an orphan whose prodigious mental powers lead to adventure.

Oliver Twist, by Charles Dickens—Perhaps the most famous orphan of all time. His mother died in childbirth. His father is gone for no apparent reason.

Peter Pan, by J.M. Barrie—Peter was lost as an infant. When he went back to see his parents, they had a new baby—so he flew away forever.

Pippi Longstocking, by Astrid Lindgren—Pippi's father was washed overboard during a particularly nasty storm.

Pollyanna, by Eleanor H. Porter—Another famous orphan from literature, Pollyanna remains hopeful in the face of ever-worsening circumstances—including the deaths of her parents. To be a Pollyanna is to be irrationally, even irritatingly, optimistic.

The Secret Garden, by Frances Hodgson Burnett—Colin's mother, Lilias, fell from a tree in the garden, triggering the premature birth of her child and ultimately her own death. Mary's mother died of cholera in India, along with Mary's father and all of the household servants.

A Series of Unfortunate Events, by Lemony Snicket—The Baudelaire siblings' parents perished in a suspicious fire in this series.

Star Wars, directed by George Lucas—Luke Skywalker's mother, Padmé, died from an appallingly literal "broken heart" shortly after childbirth. And if you don't know what happened to his father, well, congratulations.

Superman, by Jerry Siegel—The Man of Steel's parents were scientists who predicted the demise of their own planet and sent him off in a rocket to find an inhabitable planet. What great parents!

The Wizard of Oz, by L. Frank Baum—Dorothy Gale's parents died of unspecified causes. Perhaps they, too, were blown away.

First Sentences

Here are a few noteworthy novel openers:

NOTICE
Persons attempting to find a motive in this narrative will be prosecuted; persons attempting to find a moral in it will be banished; persons attempting to find a plot in it will be shot.
BY ORDER OF THE AUTHOR
—Mark Twain, *The Adventures of Huckleberry Finn*

One thing was certain, that the white kitten had nothing to do with it: —it was the black kitten's fault entirely.
—Lewis Carroll, *Through the Looking-Glass*

It was seven o'clock of a very warm evening in the Seeonee hills when Father Wolf woke up from his day's rest, scratched himself, yawned, and spread out his paws one after the other to get rid of the sleepy feeling in their tips.
—Rudyard Kipling, *The Jungle Book*

There was a boy called Eustace Clarence Scrubb, and he almost deserved it.
—C.S. Lewis, *The Voyage of the Dawn Treader*

Whether I shall turn out to be the hero of my own life, or whether that station will be held by anybody else, these pages must show.

—Charles Dickens, *David Copperfield*

If you really want to hear about it, the first thing you'll probably want to know is where I was born, and what my lousy childhood was like, and how my parents were occupied and all before they had me, and all that David Copperfield kind of crap, but I don't feel like going into it, if you want to know the truth.

—J.D. Salinger, *The Catcher in the Rye*

"Where's Papa going with that ax?"
—E.B. White, *Charlotte's Web*

What do these sentences have in common? Not much that I can see. And yet they all make me want to read more: Is that *really* what it's like to be a wolf? What did the black cat do that was so bad? Will I be shot for reading *Huckleberry Finn*? Will David Copperfield turn out to be a hero or a villain? Are there going to be more bad words in *The Catcher in the Rye* or is *crap* the worst one? What did Eustace Clarence Scrubb do to deserve to be named Eustace Clarence Scrubb? And where *is* Papa going with that ax? I thought *Charlotte's Web* was a sweet story about barnyard animals—not a murder mystery!

WRITING TIPS

Ideas: Lie, Cheat, and Steal

Where do I get my story ideas? When readers ask me this, I usually tell them I'm sorry, I don't know where my ideas come from. There is no method to my madness, just...madness. If they persist in questioning me, I tell them I don't have to come up with ideas because everything I write is true. But, I admit, these aren't very satisfying answers.

In order to get all of you budding young authors off my back, I've decided to come up with some helpful suggestions for coming up with ideas. Or at least some suggestions that sound helpful. Here's what I've got so far. Let me know what you think....

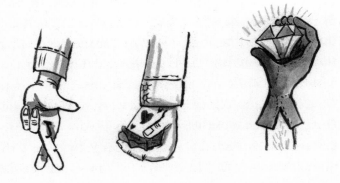

1. Lie

Lying is always your first and best option when it comes to writing fiction. Need a subject for a story? Just make it up. Whoever wrote *write what you know* obviously didn't know what they were writing. If writers only wrote what they knew, there would be no stories about fairies or dwarves or dragons. No animals would ever talk. Only murderers would write murder mysteries, and only ghosts would write ghost stories. A story starts with an act of imagination. And if your ending is half decent, it ends with one, too. A good liar is a good tale-teller. So, please, tell tall tales. The taller the better.

2. Cheat

Then again, take it from me: it's very hard to make up something new every time you sit down to write. This is what they call writer's block, and it results in a lot of hair-tearing, teeth-gnashing, and, of course, chocolate-eating. When you can't come up with something that has never happened, cheat—use something that has happened. But change it up a little. In real life, it was your brother who stuck your head in the toilet? Well, that's the great thing about fiction. Now you can stick his head in. So you didn't actually throw your book at your teacher when he called on you—this is your chance. One word of caution, however: please, please change the names of the people involved. You only want them to *suspect* you're writing about them....

3. Steal

When you're completely drawing a blank, when the wondrous wellspring of your imagination has dried up, when you've mined all your childhood memories for golden story-nuggets, then it's time to commit the ultimate authorial crime: Grand Theft Autho. In other words, steal an idea from someone else. As I once famously said, *Bad artists copy. Good artists steal.* (Actually, it was Pablo Picasso who said that, but who's counting?) Maybe you steal from a movie you saw. Or a book you liked. Or even better, a book you didn't like. But in this case you should change it up more than a little; you should change it up a lot. When I was younger, one writer might have copied another with impunity. Nowadays, with so much information at everyone's fingertips, you will almost certainly be caught. So make sure that all your words are your own and that you change the context of the idea/event/theme you are stealing. Then you will not be a plagiarist—you will be a master thief.

Say, just for instance, the movie you're stealing from concerns a friendship between a boy and an alien. Maybe you make your story about the friendship between a boy and a dragon. Oh, shoot, that's been done. How about a boy and a whale? Oops, that's been done, too. A boy and a robot ...? Oh, well, you know what I mean. In fact, there are plenty of stories to be written about aliens, dragons, whales, *and* robots. I'll tell you a secret: there are very few original ideas. (Not even the idea that there are few original ideas is original.) Most writers, even the best writers, steal all the time. In the end, the important thing is not so much where your ideas come from, but what you do with them. But that's a subject for another essay: not Lie, Cheat, and Steal but, let's see, how about Shake, Rattle, and Roll?

Class dismissed.

EAVESDROPPING

Good eavesdropping skills are vital for any writer, whether you're looking for story ideas, intriguing characters, or just a bit of dialogue. Here are some strategies and techniques writers employ to divert attention from themselves while they listen to other people's conversations.

Diversion techniques:

Staring into space
Hiding behind a book or magazine
Pretending to listen to an iPod

Places to eavesdrop:

Bus or bus stop
Restaurant, coffeehouse, cafeteria
Outside your big sister's bedroom door

Things to listen for:

Story and/or character ideas
Dialogue and/or speech patterns
Secrets

CHOOSE YOUR OWN AWARD

THE OLD-BERRY, SNOB-BERRY &
DARK-CHOCOLATE-DIPPED-STRAWBERRY
AWARD FOR EXCELLENCE IN
CHILDREN'S LITERATURE
(This is the big one.)

ACADEMY AWARD, BEST ORIGINAL MATERIAL
FOR FUTURE ADAPTED SCREENPLAY
(Hey, I'm an optimist.)

LITTLE LEAGUE REGIONAL CHAMPIONS
(Just because I never got this one.)

VALENTINE
(Never got too many
of those, either.)

*WHY WAIT FOR THE WORLD TO GIVE YOU ONE? HECK, WHY WAIT UNTIL YOU
FINISH WRITING YOUR BOOK?

TITLES FOR UNWRITTEN BOOKS

Now that you've bestowed upon yourself a well-deserved award, it's clear that you have a glittering writing career ahead of you. Celebrate by naming all the brilliant books you will write in the future—or that you will *think* about writing in the future while you are resting on your laurels (and/or while you are beset by a terrible case of writer's block). Who knows, if the titles are good enough—they might be enough.*

If you are one of those old-fashioned people who think a title should reflect the content of a book, here are some unwritten books for you to name:

---

*THE DIRECTOR PETER BOGDANOVICH ONCE ASKED ORSON WELLES WHAT HE THOUGHT OF A PROSPECTIVE TITLE FOR BOGDANOVICH'S UPCOMING FILM *PAPER MOON*. WELLES SAID, "THAT TITLE IS SO GOOD, YOU SHOULDN'T EVEN MAKE THE PICTURE; YOU SHOULD JUST RELEASE THE TITLE!"

A guide to the flora and fauna of your backyard

Title: _

A cookbook for cannibals

Title: _ _ _ _ _ _ _ _ _ _ _ _ _ _ _ _ _ _ _

A self-help book for moody cats

Title: _

A how-to manual for cat burglars

Title: _

The next Pseudonymous Bosch book
(Seriously, I need a title!)

Title: _ _ _ _ _ _ _ _ _ _ _ _ _ _ _ _ _ _

A REAL-LIVE READER INTERVIEWS
PSEUDONYMOUS BOSCH*

HOW DID YOU COME UP WITH YOUR PEN NAME?

Pseudonymous is an old family name. Bosch is the name of my dishwasher. (My toaster is called Cuisinart—that didn't seem as good.)

DO YOUR FRIENDS CALL YOU PSEUDO AS WELL?

Friends? What friends? My rabbit calls me Hey You. My cat doesn't really talk to me anymore.

WHAT/WHO INSPIRED YOU TO BECOME A WRITER AND WHY?

All my best friends are books (see above), and I'm very competitive with my friends.

WHAT ARE YOUR FAVORITE GENRES TO READ?

Mystery—for the questions. Science fiction and fantasy—for the answers. True crime—for professional advice.

*THANKS TO SPECIAL AGENT MAX MINDICH FOR THE QUESTIONS!

WHEN DID YOU START WRITING PROFESSIONALLY?

In writing, I still consider myself very much an amateur. Crime is another story....

TO YOU, WHAT IS THE HARDEST PART OF WRITING?

The part that comes before being finished.

ARE YOU A GOOD SECRET KEEPER?

I can't tell you. OK, I'll tell you. No.

LAST (AND MAYBE MOST IMPORTANT), HOW DID YOU DEVELOP YOUR LOVE FOR CHOCOLATE?

Love at first bite?

Acknowledgments[*]

---

* THE GREAT THING ABOUT BEING AN ANONYMOUS PSEUDONYMOUS AUTHOR
IS THAT I GET TO PRETEND I WRITE MY BOOKS ALL BY MYSELF. I DON'T
ACKNOWLEDGE THE HELP I RECEIVE, BECAUSE I CAN'T ACKNOWLEDGE IT; IT'S
SECRET. YOU, ALAS, HAVE NO SUCH EXCUSE. USE THIS SPACE TO THANK ALL THE
PEOPLE WHO HAVE ASSISTED YOU IN THE MAKING OF THIS BOOK. I SUGGEST
YOU START WITH ME.

Paste flattering photo of yourself here.
Tip: Eyeglasses will make you look more intellectual.

ABOUT THE AUTHOR*

* I.E., *YOU.*

WISH
YOU
WERE
HERE.

TO:

P.B., AUTHOR AT LARGE

WRITE QUICHE'S
LETTER TO P.B. HERE.